SUCH A GOOD [illegible]?

I thought of how happy I'd been only ten minutes ago at the prospect of my lazy weekend. And now Shane had come over basically telling me for the millionth time what a dull priss I was.

"Good-bye," I said loudly.

"I'm going, I'm going," he said. "The excitement in here is too much for me anyway."

I followed him through the living room, still armed with the spatula. He lingered in the doorway. "I guess it would be too much to expect you to have a party," he said mockingly. "After all, you are the principal's daughter and such a good little girl—hey—"

I pushed him bodily out the door. He stumbled out onto the porch and I slammed the heavy door shut behind him.

I turned and caught sight of myself in the hall mirror. I was the picture of fury: chalky skin, flashing eyes, lips tightened, chest heaving, brow perspiring.

Well, naturally I would look furious. I *was* furious. But somehow, as mad as I felt, I couldn't help wishing that I'd looked prettier while Shane was here.

Don't miss any of the books in Love Stories – a terrific new series of romances from Bantam Books:

Available now:

1. MY FIRST LOVE *by Callie West*
2. SHARING SAM *by Katherine Applegate*
3. HOW TO KISS A GUY *by Elizabeth Bernard*
4. THE BOY NEXT DOOR *by Janet Quin-Harkin*
5. THE DAY I MET HIM *by Catherine Clark*
6. LOVE CHANGES EVERYTHING *by ArLynn Presser*
7. MORE THAN A FRIEND *by Elizabeth Winfrey*
8. THE LANGUAGE OF LOVE *by Kate Emburg*
9. MY SO-CALLED BOYFRIEND *by Elizabeth Winfrey*
10. IT HAD TO BE YOU *by Stephanie Doyon*
11. SOME GIRLS DO *by Dahlia Kosinski*

SUPER EDITION

LISTEN TO MY HEART *by Katherine Applegate*

Love Stories

SOME GIRLS DO

DAHLIA KOSINSKI

BANTAM BOOKS
NEW YORK • TORONTO • LONDON • SYDNEY • AUCKLAND

LOVE STORIES: SOME GIRLS DO
A BANTAM BOOK : 0 553 40986 7

First publication in Great Britain

PRINTING HISTORY
Bantam edition published 1997

Cover design by Slatter Anderson

Bantam Books are published by Transworld Publishers Ltd,
61–63 Uxbridge Road, Ealing, London W5 5SA,
in Australia by Transworld Publishers (Australia) Pty Ltd,
15–25 Helles Avenue, Moorebank, NSW 2170,
and in New Zealand by Transworld Publishers (NZ) Ltd,
3 William Pickering Drive, Albany, Auckland.

Printed and bound in Great Britain by
Cox & Wyman Ltd, Reading, Berkshire.

For my parents, who loved me even when I was in high school.

The author wishes to thank Risa Goldstein, Hilary Steinitz, and Leslie Morgenstein for their patience and hand-holding; Kris Dahl and Dorothea Herrey at ICM for keeping the wolves from the door; Sara Eckel, Stan Friedman, and Jennifer Richardson for their high-school stories; Leslie Brough, Jo Keene, Clare Murphy, and Maria Ridout for their help after the Great Computer Crash; Dorothy Heiny for her readership; and Ian McCredie for his eggs Benedict.

SOME GIRLS DO

Eavesdroppers often hear highly entertaining and instructive things.

—Margaret Mitchell
Gone with the Wind

A characteristic of the Open Party is that the parents of the host are unaware that it is taking place, usually because they are out of town.

—Judith Martin
Miss Manners' Guide for the Turn-of-the-Millennium

ONE

If you've ever thought that being the principal's daughter gives you any special privileges at school, I'll put that idea to rest right now. For instance, there's the matter of Mrs. McCracken's advanced placement English class. Mrs. McCracken is one of the most unpopular teachers at Knox High School, and just about everyone who qualifies for her class manages to weasel out of it. But not me, the principal's daughter. You see, my dad is pretty proud of the entire advanced placement program, and he'd be offended if his own daughter didn't accept the honor of being admitted to it.

Well, on that beautiful Michigan Indian summer Friday, the fourth day of my senior year, sitting in Mrs. McCracken's class with five other poor slobs (who for reasons of their own couldn't get out of it either) didn't feel like any great honor.

A few details about Mrs. McCracken. She's about sixty, stout, bosomy, cotton haired, eagle-eyed, razor tongued, and generally sharp as a tack. If you tell her why you absolutely, positively can't turn your paper in on time, she fixes you with her steely gaze and says, "You have obviously mistaken me for someone who cares." Plus she refers to every author we read as "Mister." As in "Mr. Shakespeare" and "Mr. Jonson." Like they're not really famous writers, but ordinary guys who work at the bank or something. Except for Charles Dickens, whom she calls "dear Mr. Dickens." She gets a little glassy-eyed whenever she talks about him, which is a lot. I have been taking AP English with Mrs. McCracken for over three years and we have never read anything written after 1900 because whenever we hit *A Tale of Two Cities* or *Bleak House* or whatever, Mrs. McCracken says, "Oh, class, dear Mr. Dickens was so talented, I just can't bring myself to move on yet. Shall we read *Great Expectations*?" and so on until summer vacation.

"All right, class, please open Mr. Homer's text to line 137," Mrs. McCracken said, sharply tapping her pencil on her desk. "Who would like to begin reading?"

I sighed. Somehow I had the feeling that my senior year would be pretty much a drag. It wasn't only the thought of AP English and its never-changing reading list. It was me, Melanie Merrill, and my never-changing social life. On the popular-unpopular scale, I guess I'm pretty much in the middle. This means that I've always managed to muster up a date to the prom, but never to the Fall Ball. Truly popular girls get asked to *every* dance. For instance, my best friend since kindergarten, Katie Crimson, has gone to about five hundred dances since she was, oh, twelve. I must admit, being best friends with someone so popular has lent me a certain amount of respectability.

Yes, I'm respectable, but I don't exactly sparkle in any particular way. I mean, I don't have a boyfriend and I don't run with a particular crowd. Most people look at me as the principal's daughter—as permanent and inevitable a school fixture as the bathroom sinks but no more exciting. In fact, even though I'm not a straight-A student, or a snitch, or compulsively obedient, I've sort of got this reputation for being incredibly, dully *good.* Sometimes I think that just comes with the territory when you're the principal's daughter; I'd basically have to go around making bomb scares and cheating on tests before people would start believing I wasn't some goody-goody.

But I couldn't help hoping that maybe this year would be different. Maybe I would stop being Melanie Merrill, principal's daughter, and start being popular or beautiful or sociable. Maybe . . .

"Melanie Merrill," Mrs. McCracken said, breaking into my thoughts. "Would you be so kind as to read aloud to us?"

Another bad thing about Mrs. McCracken. The way she always says *Would you be so kind?* or *Do you mind favoring us?* It's her way of rubbing it in that we're students and even though we *do* mind, we can't say so because we're being graded.

I opened my copy of *The Odyssey* and began reading out loud. Actually, I don't mind it all that much. It's not that stressful because everyone else is just following along in their texts. Also, teachers never call on you after you're done because you've already participated enough.

The classroom windows were open, and the warm September breeze puffed at the window shades. I listened to my own voice ebb and flow with the rhythm of the words. I reached the part where Odysseus and the gang poke out the Cyclops's eye:

> Then, heaving together, we raised it up
> and brought it down with all our might
> into the sleeping giant's eye. It hissed as
> when a blacksmith quenches hot iron—

THUNK!

My voice cracked and I practically jumped out

of my skin since the thump had come from right behind me. I turned around in my seat and saw Brad Hopkins, captain of the football team, lying on the floor with his eyes closed and a huge goose egg forming on his temple.

"Good heavens!" snapped Mrs. McCracken from the lectern. "Mr. Hopkins, will you kindly resume your seat?"

Brad's eyelids fluttered, but he didn't wake up.

Robin Christiansen, who was sitting next to Brad, raised her hand. "Mrs. McCracken? Brad's fainted."

Mrs. McCracken frowned. She walked around her desk and over to where she could see Brad better.

"Oh, my!" she said softly.

She bustled down the aisle and knelt next to him. "Bradley?" She patted his cheek. "Bradley, are you okay?"

Brad groaned. He opened his eyes and saw Mrs. McCracken. He closed his eyes again.

"Bradley?" Mrs. McCracken's voice grew sharper. "Bradley, wake up!"

He heaved a huge sigh and spoke, his eyes still shut. "I . . . think I fainted."

Mrs. McCracken sighed also. "I can see that," she said. "What's the matter? Didn't you eat breakfast this morning?"

Brad swallowed. "No. I mean, yes, I ate breakfast. It was just—just hearing about—about the eye and the hot poker—" He swallowed again.

Mrs. McCracken sat back on her heels. She patted Brad's hand. "There, there, Bradley," she said briskly. "No need to dwell on it. Would you like to go to Nurse Carlin's office?"

He nodded.

"Can you walk?"

He nodded.

Mrs. McCracken's lips twitched faintly. "I think it might help if you opened your eyes, Bradley." She stood up. "Melanie, if you'll be so generous as to walk Bradley to Nurse Carlin's office since it was your impassioned reading that seemed to get to him." She strode back to the front of the room, her heels clicking.

I helped Brad to his feet and we walked slowly out in the hall. As we left, I heard Mrs. McCracken saying, "Now, class, I believe we've all just witnessed the power of truly great literature."

I rolled my eyes. I could see the question on the final exam now: *Which powerful lines from* The Odyssey *caused Bradley Hopkins to faint?*

Brad rubbed at his temple.

I tried not to stare at the painful-looking lump over his eye. "You okay?" I asked softly.

He blew out a breath and smiled. "Yeah, I will be, I guess."

We walked along in silence. Brad Hopkins is the school's star athlete and very handsome in this kind of huge-bodied, heavy-featured way.

Probably a lot of girls would be really thrilled to escort him anywhere, even to the office. But I've known Brad since kindergarten. It wasn't thrilling to me, it was just more of what I was used to: Brad in his role as popular guy, me in my role as helpful principal's daughter.

We paused in the doorway of the office. Nurse Carlin and the secretary, Mrs. Zimmerman, were talking to a boy I'd never seen before.

He was a pretty typical-looking guy, thin, wearing jeans and a T-shirt with a ragged flannel shirt over it. His light brown hair was short and straight but a little unruly, like maybe he'd been running his hands through it while he waited for the incredibly slow Mrs. Zimmerman to take care of him. It wasn't until he turned to look at us that I saw his eyes. They were a clear bright sparkling green, with long brown lashes. On a girl they would have been gorgeous, but on a guy, they were—well, *piercing.* The boy looked at me and an expression I didn't quite understand crossed his face.

"Brad Hopkins!" Nurse Carlin exclaimed. "What happened to you?"

Brad touched the bump on his forehead. "It's a long story," he said. "Could I just lie down on the cot for a while?"

"Sure," Nurse Carlin said, taking his arm. "Nicolette Dunlap is lying on it right now, but she just has cramps. We can make her move."

The new boy smiled and I cringed. Well, so much for Nicolette's privacy!

I watched Nurse Carlin lead Brad away and then I turned to go.

"Just a minute, Melanie," Mrs. Zimmerman said. "This is Knox High's newest student." She turned to the new guy. "This is Melanie Merrill, our principal's daughter. She'll walk you to class."

I tried to smile at the new guy casually, but I could have killed Mrs. Zimmerman. *Melanie Merrill, our principal's daughter.* Didn't I even get a chance to establish some sort of identity of my own?

Mrs. Zimmerman smiled. "First we have to fill out a few forms. Now, young man—" She shuffled some papers. "Your name is Shawn?"

"Shane," said the new guy.

"Shane?"

"Yeah. SHANE. Like the western? My mother loves that old movie, you know, the one with Alan Ladd?"

Mrs. Zimmerman's eyes sparkled. "You don't have to tell me who's in *Shane*, young man. I must have seen that movie seventeen times when I was a girl. Alan Ladd was wonderful in it; so handsome and masculine." She sighed.

Shane grinned. "My mother thought so too," he said wryly. "But I'm not sure that's a good enough reason to name your firstborn after him."

Right away I felt a lot of sympathy for this

guy. I have younger sisters named Pride and Joy, and I had a sudden vision of what life was going to be like for them, filling out routine forms and having to give a lot of explanations to strangers. Thank heavens my parents had me while they were still too young and unsure of themselves to go out on a limb namewise.

Mrs. Zimmerman finished filling out Shane's forms. She never lets students fill out their own forms because she says she can't read their handwriting. My father says she writes everything in code so that she'll be indispensable and he won't be able to fire her. Of course, if that's true, the whole school system will grind to a screeching halt when she retires.

Mrs. Zimmerman nibbled the end of her pen and looked over the paperwork. Then she extended her hand to Shane. "Welcome to Knox High School, Shane Conner." She gestured to me. "Melanie will show you where your locker is and walk you to your first class, which is . . ." She shuffled some more papers "Advanced placement English with Mrs. McCracken."

Lucky Shane, I thought.

Mrs. McCracken handed Shane about twenty textbooks and a million sheets of paper. Shane and I walked out into the hall.

"So I just met your dad," Shane said conversationally.

I looked at him out of the corner of my eye. I

had kind of been hoping that Shane had had his "welcome" meeting with the assistant principal, Mr. Weller. But then I remembered that Mr. Weller was at a weekend-long conference in Grand Rapids, which I knew about because his son Bobby was having a party tonight.

I decided to change the subject. "Here, let me help you with some of that," I said. I took a few textbooks and the pile of papers from him. I looked at the slip of paper with Shane's locker number on it. "Um, your locker's in the south wing. I'll show you and you can drop off your books or whatever."

Shane looked amused. "Wow, you sound so . . . professional when you say that. Authoritative yet casual. Like you show people to their lockers all the time. Are you, like, a regular student?"

"What do you mean?"

"Do you go to school here or is this your job? Are you, like, the student ambassador or something?"

"Oh, come on." I wrinkled my nose. "Of course I go to school here."

"Well, you never know," Shane said. "I thought maybe you were already out of high school and your dad, being principal, gave you this job."

I stared at him. Was he kidding?

"I mean, parents like to help their kids get jobs, you know?" Shane went on. "Listen to this.

One summer I worked as a cashier at this 7-Eleven and I was about to get fired because I couldn't work the cash register fast enough. Besides, I was giving away all sorts of freebies to my friends, so it was kind of hard to make it all balance out anyway. But *my parents* got this toy cash register out of the attic, and every night I stood behind the cash register and they filed by me pretending to buy groceries out of our own kitchen."

I frowned. "What does that have to do with—"

"Well, I thought maybe your dad wanted to, you know, help you out. Professionally, that is. Send you on your way. And I must say, you're doing a fine job. Like you were *born* to be the principal's assistant or something."

My face burned. "I don't—I don't remember asking your opinion!" I stammered.

Shane's eyes widened with surprise. "Hey, what are you getting so upset about? You can't blame me for wondering why you aren't in class."

"Look, I just happened to walk Brad to the office," I snapped. "That doesn't make me a one-person Welcome Wagon."

"Brad is that guy who looks like someone clubbed him over the head with a frying pan?"

"Uh-huh," I told him, relieved to be talking about something besides my abilities as student ambassador. We began climbing the south stairs.

"Is he your boyfriend?"

I couldn't help laughing. "Brad Hopkins? Yeah, right. He's—" I stopped, blushing furiously. The idea of my going out with Brad Hopkins *was* pretty outlandish, but this guy certainly didn't need to know that.

"I guess it must be hard to date when you're the principal's daughter," Shane said thoughtfully.

I bristled. "Why do you say that?"

"Oh, I guess . . ." Shane still looked pensive. "Well, the principal's daughter at my old school also happened to be my age and she was this, like, incredibly mousy person and—well, this is a really horrible story, but she went to the prom with her uncle. She thought nobody knew who he was, but she didn't fool anyone."

My blood pressure must've jumped about a hundred points in two seconds. We reached the top of the stairs. I clenched my hands into fists so hard that I left crescents on my palms. "You are so rude, obnoxious—"

He looked startled. "Hey, I'm not saying—"

"You're comparing me to some mousy girl who has to date her relatives!" I shouted. I couldn't believe this. Ten minutes ago I'd been hoping that this school year I might actually shine just a little bit, and this guy comes along and basically tells me it's hopeless—that I'm nothing more than the principal's mousy daughter.

"I wasn't comparing you," Shane protested. "I

was just saying that it must be hard being the principal's daughter on top of your, like, five million other problems."

My heart froze. "I don't have five million problems."

"I didn't mean *you.* I meant—"

"My only problem," I said in a loud clear voice, "is that I've wasted too much time being insulted by you."

I slammed the textbooks I was carrying into his arms. He stumbled a little and dropped two of them. I didn't wait for him to pick them up. Furious, I threw his stack of paperwork up in the air and stomped down the stairs in a blizzard of falling white paper.

TWO

LATER THAT AFTERNOON I sat on the open sill of the kitchen window, staring out at the street, waiting for my family to get ready so we could all go out to dinner together, which we do every Friday night. I was beginning to feel a little too old for these dinners. I mean, when *I* saw someone my age eating dinner with his or her parents on a weekend night, I always made a bazillion assumptions about how that person had no social life whatsoever.

Besides, everyone I know is a little embarrassed by her family, and I think I'm more embarrassed than most people. Don't get me wrong. I love my family and everything, but I have to say, they're a little on the weird side. I'll give you some basic information, starting with me, Melanie Merrill, even though I'm by far the least weird of the bunch: sixteen, brown eyes, light brown hair, pale skin, normal body. People are always debating what my "best feature" is, which should give you an idea of what I look like, since really attractive people are always just that—really attractive, without this nonsense about best features. Like my best friend, Katie, for example. She's petite and blond, with a little elfin haircut, and everyone says she's "darling" or "lovely" and leaves it at that.

Katie says she would give anything to have my hair, but then again, she's my best friend; she has to say things like that. If you ask me, there's nothing that spectacular about my hair, except that I've been growing it for about a decade. Anyway, my mother says my best feature is my "porcelain" complexion, but in reality that just means that I have exceptionally white skin. (Once at the beach this guy lying on a towel next to me thanked me, saying that my skin was probably *reflecting* the sun and thus helping his tan. But that's another story.) Sometimes my mother changes her mind and says that my eyes are my best feature, because they're very large. Yeah, well, you should see the family photographs where I always look like a startled deer or a mass murderer.

Okay. Next there are my twin sisters, Pride and Joy, age nine. How or why the names, I will never understand. Even my parents can't keep the story straight. Sometimes they say it has to do with my mother's maiden name being Joyce Pryde. Sometimes they say that it's because they had the name Joy all picked out and then they went to the hospital and—surprise!—there were two babies and Pride just seemed to go with Joy. Personally I think they were planning on telling people, "We named them Pride and Joy because they *are* our pride and joy." But too late they realized how that would sound with me standing there. I mean, if the new babies were their pride and joy, what did that make *me*?

Anyway, Pride and Joy are, thankfully, not identical. The last thing they need is matching outfits. Joy is soft and blond, like our mother, and very shy. Pride is dark haired, with pigtails and freckles, and it's possible that she was born talking. Sometimes when I'm away from them, I try to remember what Joy's voice sounds like and I can't. It's not because Joy talks so little, though. I think it's because Pride talks so much.

Then there's my eleven-month-old sister, Charity. When people ask about *her* name, my mother smiles wryly and says, "We named her Charity because it didn't seem very kind to name her 'Impulse' or 'Poor Judgment' or 'We Were Hoping for a Boy.'" She can say things like that about Charity because Charity is so heart-stoppingly, breathtakingly beautiful that you know just by looking at her that no one would ever wish she were a boy. She's all blond ringlets and giant blue eyes and sweet baby skin. Once an advertising executive saw her in the supermarket and arranged for my parents to bring her in to audition for baby food commercials. Unfortunately, before the audition my mother saw a segment on *60 Minutes* about how they treat children in commercials and nixed the whole deal. But anyway, that's how gorgeous Charity is. Plus she's very sweet and sunny and we're all crazy about her.

My mother is quite gorgeous herself. If you saw her wheeling Charity's stroller through the park, you would probably think she was twenty-seven instead of thirty-seven and that Charity was her first baby. She's tall and slender, with chin-length wavy blond hair and beautiful blue eyes, the kind that are so deep set that they're practically navy. Plus she has high cheekbones and a great smile. Just seeing her, you can understand why my father, who is twenty years older, eloped with her just two *days* after she graduated from high school, risking his job as a teacher and causing a gigantic scandal.

It's a little harder to understand (just from looking, I mean) why my mother ran off with my father. As I said, he's twenty years older, fifty-seven, and he pretty much looks like a high-school principal: square jaw, dark hair graying at the temples, out-of-date horn-rimmed glasses, super posture, never a hair out of place. Actually

I'm glad he's so fastidious. It would break my heart if I ever saw him walking down the hall with his pants leg caught in the top of his sock or something.

But that's just appearances. If you *met* my parents, you would understand how they must have been drawn to each other because if there are two more naive, less hip people than my parents, I can't imagine who they are. For example, my father, who spends forty hours every week in the company of over a thousand teenagers, and my mother, who used to illustrate children's books, have not grasped the concept of popular and unpopular.

For instance, every year my father invites the top ten students in the senior class over for a barbecue. Now, needless to say, any popular person who finds himself in the Top Ten quickly finds an excuse not to come. But the unpopular people—the math nerds, the science geeks, the boys in starched shirts, the girls in blouses and thick glasses—they all come! They bring my mother flowers! And they stay and stay, talking away to my parents until we practically have to push them out the door. And then, as my parents are cleaning up, one of them *invariably* says to the other, "Why, what a nice group of teenagers they are!" and the other says, "Yes indeed, but didn't you get the sense that they're a little lonely?" and the first one says, "Oh, did you think that too? I can't imagine why; they're all so smart."

Now can you believe that? *They're all so smart!* As if being as smart as those kids are wouldn't almost automatically drum you out of the popular circle. I mean, last year this one kid spent an hour and forty-five minutes telling my mother all about this miniature castle he's building out of matchsticks. And she wonders why a nice bright boy like that isn't at the top of every high-school girl's wish list. . . .

Sitting in the window, I sighed and shook my head. What could I do? They were my family and I loved them. I could hardly refuse to appear in public with them. Besides, I said to myself, it wasn't like I had no social life. I was, in fact, right this minute waiting for Katie to call me so we could talk about what to wear to Bobby Weller's party.

I glanced at my watch. Katie was supposed to call twenty minutes ago, when she got home from cheerleading practice.

A movement across the street caught my eye. Someone passed by a window of the Jamesons' house, which was odd, since the Jamesons moved out two months ago.

"Mom!" I shouted.

"What, honey?" my mother's voice drifted down the stairs.

"Did someone move into the Jamesons'?"

"Yes!" she called impatiently. She hates to have shouted conversations. "The moving van was there yesterday."

I studied the house across the street, wondering who lived there. Maybe they would have a kid my age—someone cool, I hoped. It suddenly occurred to me that whoever lived in the Jamesons' was probably tying up the phone, because we have a party line.

I'm sure I have to explain what a party line is because most people under the age of fifty have never heard of them. But my father believes that having a party line is a great way to save money on the phone bill. If it were up to me, I'd choose to save money by buying, say, generic-brand peanut butter, but we've had a party line for as long as I can remember, so I'm pretty used to it.

The basic idea is that we share a phone line with the house across the street. I'm not sure how this works technically; all I know is that sometimes when you picked up the phone, instead of a dial tone you could hear Mr. Jameson droning on about his bursitis to one of his friends, and then you had to put down the receiver and wait until he finished. And sometimes when *Mr. Jameson* picked up the phone, he could hear me chattering away to Katie, saying, "Okay, then I said, fine, and then he said—" at which point Mr. Jameson would interrupt and say, "Will you girls please save your gossip for another time? I have to place an emergency call." Now how many times in his life did he have to place an emergency call? Surely not all the times he said he did, I can guarantee. Nobody—

The phone startled me out of my reverie.

"Hello?"

"Melanie?" Katie said. "I've been trying to call you for half an hour and your line's been busy."

"I think our new neighbors are on our party line," I said.

"Oh, jeez," Katie said. "I thought that when the Jamesons moved away, we were done with that business."

"Well, my dad says the phone company's supposed to notify us if the new people want to cancel the party line," I explained. "No word so far."

Katie sighed. I think she's more irritated by the party line than I am. "Anyway, what are you wearing tonight?"

"I don't know," I said. "Maybe my green sweater."

"Oh, you look fantastic in that."

"You say that about whatever I wear," I said.

"I do not," Katie said indignantly. "I don't say it about that shirt with the horizontal stripes. The one where you can see the outline of your bra clear as day?"

"Oh, I'd like to see *that,*" a strange guy's voice on the line said.

Both Katie and I were stunned into silence for a moment. Then Katie said, "Mel?" in a very soft voice.

"I'm still here," I whispered back.

"It's not going to do any good to whisper," the voice said. "I mean, it's not like you can whisper into each other's *ears*. Whatever you say is still going to travel along the same phone line."

I stood up straighter, even though I was alone in the kitchen. "Sir," I said in my most dignified voice. "This is a private conversation."

"You could have fooled me," the guy replied. His voice was faintly familiar, but I couldn't place it exactly. "All I did was pick up my phone and there you were. That doesn't sound very—"

"Sir, please hang up," I said firmly.

"Hey, I haven't even found out what Katie's wearing yet," he protested.

I sighed in exasperation. "Katie," I said loudly. "I will talk to you later."

"Okay," she said, and we hung up.

I wandered back to the window and glared venomously at the house across the street. So much for my hopes that the new neighbors would have a cool kid. What a jerk that guy was.

Movement caught my eye. A figure had appeared in one of the windows in the Jamesons' old house, a scrap of white in its hand. I squinted but couldn't make anything out. I turned quickly and rummaged in a kitchen drawer for my mother's bird-watching binoculars.

When I turned back to the window, the figure was still standing there. I raised the binoculars to my eyes, and then my hands began shaking so much that I nearly dropped them.

The scrap of white was a hand-lettered sign that said HI, MELANIE. The figure holding it and waving cheerily at me was Shane Conner.

Okay, so Shane Conner, the guy who rudely and obnoxiously branded me as the dull, mousy principal's daughter the moment he set foot in Knox High, was living across the street. So he was sharing a party line with my family. I was not about to let those facts ruin the rest of senior year—or even that one night. I managed to block Shane out of my mind through dinner with my family. And when we arrived home after dinner, I began getting ready for Bobby Weller's party. I put on a short black lace dress that Katie brought me from San Francisco. Normally I don't wear dresses. I usually stick to jeans and sweaters, but I liked this dress, and the party seemed like a good excuse to wear it. Besides, I was trying to change my image, right?

Of course, I reminded myself, I wasn't so pathetic that I desperately *needed* to change my image. I mean, it's not like I've never been on a date. My romantic history isn't exactly earth shattering, but I do have *some* experience. In fact, the first date I ever went on was when I was twelve years old and it was with—brace yourself—this nineteen-year-old *sailor* who was painting our house for extra money during shore leave or whatever they call it. Actually, it's not quite as shocking as it sounds because my parents didn't know it was a date or they wouldn't have let me go, and I didn't know it was a date or I wouldn't have gone. My parents and I both thought the sailor—his name was Jerry—was taking me to the movies, a matinee, with his little sister. (In reality, he was only taking me to a movie his little sister had seen.)

Anyway, Jerry seemed fairly sure we were on a date because as soon as we got to the theater, he steered me into the back row and put his arm around me. He said, "I really like you, Melanie." I said, "I really like you too," because that seemed like the polite thing to say. Then, before the movie even *started,* he gave me this huge wet kiss. I was shocked. I think Jerry sensed that he'd gone too far and he didn't kiss me again, although he did call me at eleven o'clock that night and say, "Hey, what did you think of my kiss?" and I said, "Not much," and he never called again.

So then I basically devoted the next four years to my crush on Ben Crimson. Ben is Katie's older brother. He's as popular and good looking as she is, and I liked him almost the instant we met, way back in grade school. All freshman and sophomore year I tried very hard never to let it show—I figured there was no possible way he'd like me back, and Katie would probably get all embarrassingly protective of me.

Then the most unbelievable thing happened. Ben asked me to the prom my sophomore year. It was, like, the greatest day of my life, romantically speaking. Ben kissed me good night and told me that he'd liked me for a long time, but he'd felt funny, liking one of Katie's friends. Sheesh, if only we'd known this sooner! Anyway, Ben graduated two weeks later and got shipped off to Notre Dame for a summer of football practice before the school year began. When I saw him at Christmas, he was dating about half of the cheerleading team and was way too cool for the likes of a high-school junior such as me.

After Ben, I was basically crush-free. I went to the junior prom with this guy named Jon Stillerman, whose father is the chemistry teacher. We had a good enough time at the prom and even went out a few times after that, but somehow the sparks weren't there. Plus there was something just a little too *much* about the principal's daughter dating the chemistry teacher's son.

I finished dressing for Bobby's party, then went into the kitchen. Katie was already there, talking to my parents. She was wearing jeans and a red velvet shirt. Her wonderful short corn silk hair shone in the lamplight.

"Hey, you're wearing the dress I gave you," she said, pleased.

I hugged my elbows, suddenly self-conscious. "Do I look all dressed up and pathetic?"

"You look fabulous, sweetie," my mother assured me.

"You really do look great," Katie agreed. "Let's go."

"Where are you going?" my father asked.

"To a party at, uh, the Johnsons' house," I said, making up a name at random. If my father knew we were going to the Wellers', he might get very nervous, knowing that Mr. and Mrs. Weller were in Grand Rapids.

"You're going to a party at ten o'clock?" he said. That's another thing he doesn't understand about teenagers—how we're practically nocturnal.

Finally we left my house and began walking the few blocks to the Wellers' house. We weren't halfway there before we could hear the music. "I guess this means it'll be a loud one," Katie remarked.

"I hope the sound doesn't reach my parents," I joked. "They might wonder what's going on and take a walk to investigate."

We approached the Wellers' sedate brick house, which was almost visibly throbbing with music and laughter and shouted conversation. Bobby Weller was standing on the front porch, smoking a clove cigarette. Bobby doesn't deal all that well with the pressure of being the child of a school faculty member. He smokes and drinks and runs around with all the burnouts. Still, I kind of like him in spite of myself. The same goes for the teachers, I guess, because they keep passing him even though he never does any homework. The whole school is in a kindly conspiracy to keep this from Mr. Weller, who is one of those painfully naive people and probably wouldn't believe it anyway.

"Hi, Bobby," I said.

"Hi, Mel." He smiled in his vague, dopey way. "Hi, Katie. Go on in."

We fought our way through the crowd to the kitchen. There were a bazillion empty bottles littering every surface of the room.

The only thing left to drink was bright red punch in a very smudged and fingerprint-covered glass bowl. Katie and I ladled out two cups. I tasted it. "Kool-Aid?"

Katie sipped and nodded. "But knowing Bobby, I suspect it's not *just* Kool-Aid."

I took another taste. "You're probably right, but it's so sweet, I can't tell."

Katie saw someone she knew in the corner of the kitchen and went over to say hello. I was adding some fruit juice to my cup when a voice from behind me said, "That doesn't look like a green sweater."

I turned around. Shane Conner had pulled a

chair over to the Wellers' refrigerator and was sitting in front of the open door, surveying the contents. I pushed my bangs off my forehead, feeling flustered. "I decided not to wear that," I said coolly.

"Obviously." Shane opened a jar of black olives and offered it to me. I shook my head. "Did you call Katie back and tell her you changed your mind about the sweater? Why do girls do that, anyway? And are you going to throw away the striped shirt Katie was talking about?" He looked at me closely. "I can't see the outline of your bra in that dress, by the way. Or aren't you wearing one?"

Before I could think of some cutting response, Swiss Kriss wandered into the kitchen and gave Shane a soft, bright smile. Shane offered the jar of olives to her.

I have to explain that Swiss Kriss is the prettiest, most popular girl in school. Her name, obviously, isn't really Swiss Kriss. It's actually Krista Snowden, but a few years ago she had a boyfriend who drank a lot of hot cocoa. He began calling Krista Swiss Kriss after Swiss Miss, the girl on the hot cocoa box. The name stuck. Now, at the beginning of every year, when teachers call role and say, "Krista Snowden?" she raises her hand and says, "I'd like to be called Swiss Kriss, please."

She always wears her long blond hair in braids, and of course every Halloween she dresses up as

Swiss Miss, complete with lederhosen. Even when it's not Halloween, she tends to dress a lot like Swiss Miss: Peter Pan collars, suspenders, short plaid skirts, sometimes knee socks. Oh, occasionally she wears jeans and some sort of plaid flannel shirt for a more rugged look, but she never strays far from the mountaintop theme.

It goes pretty much without saying that Swiss Kriss is practically the most beautiful girl in the world—small, even features, slim nose, dark blue eyes, long black lashes, red lips, creamy skin, petite frame . . . you get the picture.

And she's exceptionally poised. She has to be to get away with the Swiss Kriss business.

Now she gave Shane another radiant smile, showing her pearly little baby teeth. "Thanks, but I'm trying to cut down."

"I know what you mean," Shane replied. "I had a terrible problem a few years back. But now I'm basically just a party olive eater."

Swiss Kriss laughed as she moved away with a swish of her dirndl skirt.

I felt a flicker of jealousy. But why would I be jealous of Swiss Kriss and Shane? I guess Swiss Kriss is just one of those people who brings out the jealousy in me.

Shane looked at me. "Melanie, someone's trying to get past you," he said. He slipped a hand around my waist and pulled me gently out of the way.

I felt a strange flutter in my stomach. I was suddenly conscious of the thinness of this lace dress. His hand was warm and firm. Then Candace Miller passed, and Shane let go.

He stuck a black olive onto each of his fingers and smiled mischievously. "Did you enjoy dinner with your parents?"

"Yes, I did," I told him, still feeling the warmth from his hand on my waist. Then I frowned. "How did you know about that?"

"I saw you. I was having dinner with some guys from school."

I cringed inwardly. So Shane got to see the principal's daughter and immediate family wholesomely breaking bread together on a Friday night. I'm sure he must think I'm an even bigger dud than he had in the first place. I could see it now—Shane and his table full of friends pointing and snickering at the sight of me with my family.

And how did he make friends so quickly anyway? He'd been at Knox High for exactly one day and already he was having dinner with some guys from school?

I crossed my arms. "You sound like you've never eaten a meal with your parents."

Shane began eating the olives from his fingers. "Not in a—restaurant—on a weekend night." His green eyes danced. "I'd be afraid that everyone's staring at me, wondering what kind of loser has dinner with his parents instead of his friends."

So he had been mocking me! "I don't have to listen to this," I said, and brushed past him just as he began to attack a plate of fried chicken.

I walked to the corner of the kitchen where Katie was talking to Alex Chase and Marty Richards, two popular and good-looking, but totally hyper, guys from school. Whenever I see them I think of lima beans, because when they were twelve, Marty shoved a lima bean up Alex's nose and Alex had to have it surgically removed.

"What did the doctor say to the kid who complained that nobody paid any attention to him?" Alex was saying to Katie.

Katie smiled indulgently. "What?"

"Next!" Alex shouted, and Marty laughed.

I sighed. "I'm leaving," I said to Katie. "You can stay if you want."

"What's wrong? Did that new kid say something to you?"

"No. I just want to go."

Marty gave me a knowing look. "Tired, huh? I guess you're not really a late-night person."

I glared at him. Marty's basically harmless, but he definitely comes from the Melanie's-the-principal's-daughter-therefore-she-must-be-a-total-good-girl school. I do my best to ignore him.

Katie ignored him too. "Well, I'll go with you," she said, looking a little puzzled. "Why don't you sleep over at my house? We need to study together tomorrow anyway."

We were just walking out the kitchen door when we met Mr. and Mrs. Weller coming in. They had dazed, horrified looks on their faces. I wondered what had happened to their plans to stay overnight in Grand Rapids.

Luckily I don't think Mr. Weller noticed me. He was looking at Shane, who was nibbling at the last drumstick.

"Son," Mr. Weller said, "that chicken was for our Sunday dinner."

Of course, the Wellers' arrival caused a mass exodus and I was crushed against the wall by the stampede. Swiss Kriss was right in front of me and she paused suddenly, looking over her shoulder. I followed her glance.

Shane was smiling at us, his green eyes dancing merrily. He waved the drumstick good-bye with a flourish. And in the next instant, as the crowd carried me out the door, I felt an unexpected tingle up my spine. Could just a fraction of that flourish have been meant for me?

THREE

I'M SURE YOU know a teacher or faculty member who is always sullen, speaks only in a monotone, and never makes eye contact with students. Well, you may not know it, but there's a technical term for that behavior: psychological burnout. When people spend forty or more hours a week being made fun of and lied to by teenagers, they are strong candidates for burnout.

Which brings me to Doc Ellis. Doc Ellis has possibly the worst case of psychological burnout ever recorded, which is not surprising, considering that he was teaching geometry not only twenty years ago, when my mother was studying the subject, but twenty years before *that,* when my father was in high school as well! That should give you an idea of how old Doc Ellis is. His suits seem to have been around a few generations too.

You know the kind I mean: stained, rumpled, frayed cuffs, wide lapels? Okay, okay, I know I shouldn't judge him by his lack of fashion sense, and as a matter of fact, I don't have to—I can judge him by his personality, which is, in a word, unbearable.

Not only does he have the aforementioned burnout from teaching high school for too long (*decades* too long), but he never wanted to be a high-school teacher in the first place. He wanted to be a college professor, but his doctoral thesis was rejected (or so the legend goes), which is why everyone calls him "Doc" in this mildly sarcastic way. He gets revenge by being as irritable as possible and by giving excessively hard tests.

The first excessively hard test was scheduled for the second week of school. At the beginning of the hour, Doc passed out the exam and the scratch paper. "You may commence flunking," he announced in his weary, caustic voice. Then he grabbed his pack of cigarettes and went out into the hall to smoke. (I told you he suffers from psychological burnout.)

I exchanged hopeful glances with Katie across the room. We're both terrible at math, so we'd spent practically the whole weekend studying for this test. At least, it felt like the whole weekend—probably it was more like three or four hours. Still, we had worked so hard that for once I didn't feel like I was doomed.

I solved the first three problems rapidly, caught myself making a mistake on the fourth, and corrected it. I was concentrating so hard that I became aware only gradually that everyone was giggling and shifting around. I looked up, disoriented, to see Shane Conner shuffling through the papers on Doc Ellis's lectern.

I frowned and looked across at Katie, but she looked as confused as I was.

Shane found what he was looking for and cleared his throat. He tugged on the collar of his rugby shirt until it was splayed out like Doc's out-of-style dress shirts. "You may commence cheating now," he said in Doc Ellis's raspy you-people-are-the-bane-of-my-existence voice. And then he read the answers to the test.

I heard an immediate scratching of pencils, but I was too stunned to move. It wasn't that I hadn't encountered cheating before. It's practically an art form at Knox High. But this was so—blatant.

And I had studied so hard! I felt a knot forming in my stomach at the thought of all the work I'd put in over the weekend. All those wasted hours.

"For those of you who are too slow-witted to get things the first time around," Shane droned on in Doc Ellis's voice, "let me repeat myself. Forty-eight degrees, 253 square feet, five degrees . . ."

It was a good imitation, I had to admit, but I wanted to kill Shane anyway.

I was still brooding two hours later as I trudged down the hall toward the cafeteria. Shane Conner was leaning against my locker like a bad dream. Actually, as I got closer, I realized that it was Candace Miller's locker he was leaning against.

"Hey, Melanie," he said.

"Don't you start with me," I said bitterly. I spun my combination and threw open the metal door so furiously that he jumped back.

"Are you mad at me again?" he asked.

"More like *still*," I muttered.

"Oh, come on . . . ," he said. "I promise I won't tease you anymore about being the student ambassador or your dad being principal. What can I do to make it up to you? Do you want to hear the story about the time *my* dad came to school on Career Day and no one would go to his booth?"

I looked at him, surprised. "What does he do?"

"Ha! I knew you'd be interested," Shane said smugly. "He's a dermatologist."

"Forget I asked," I snapped, furious that he had distracted me. "I could kill you for cheating in geometry." I bristled just thinking about it. "I know you're new here and you probably want everyone to think you're really cool or whatever, but maybe you could think about other people once in a while, like people who studied really hard for that test or—"

"Is that what you think?" Shane raised an eyebrow at me. "That I was trying to be cool?"

I threw my books in my locker. "Oh, I'm sorry," I said sarcastically. "I guess I'm being horribly unfair to a guy who gets the whole class cheating—"

Shane's mouth twisted. "Why are you so self-righteous? You want to hear my side of the story? How does that sound?"

I slammed my locker door and folded my arms over my chest. "I'm listening."

"Yeah, and with a really open mind, I can see by your expression."

I pressed my lips together tightly as I examined him. In the few days that I'd known him, I'd come to think of Shane as a perpetual goofball—a guy who couldn't take *anything* seriously. But now something I hadn't seen before flickered in his green eyes. He actually looked *hurt*. Hurt by me? Did he really care that I was ticked off at him, that maybe I wasn't his most receptive audience?

I took a deep breath and tried to look as open-minded as possible. "All right. I really am listening."

Shane smiled faintly. I couldn't help noticing how his eyes lit up. "Okay. When I was in the office this morning giving Mrs. Zimmerman my old school records, I heard the girl that works in the office, what's her name? Angela something?"

I raised an eyebrow. "Angela Oliver?"

"Yeah, her. Anyway, she was telling this other girl about a jam she had just cleared from the Xerox machine. Then she pulled this ball of wadded-up paper out of her pocket and said that it was a copy of Doc Ellis's test. She must be in his sixth-hour class."

I looked at him steadily. "Angela isn't smart enough to solve all those problems and get the right answers." (That may sound unfeeling, but you have to trust me.)

Shane threw up his hands. "I know! She said she was going to pay William Emmett to do it during study hall and then give all the answers to her friends."

I bit my lip. That had the ring of truth to it. William Emmett is this sort of smartsy, dubious character who's good at math and probably would solve a contraband math test for five dollars or so. But that didn't exactly let Shane off the hook. "You still didn't have to give the answers to *our* class."

Shane shrugged. "No, I could have ratted on Angela Oliver and looked forward to life as an outcast here at good old Knox High."

"Well, I'm not saying—" I broke off. I couldn't argue with him. There was no question that ratting was a dangerous business. "But still—"

"Think how much more fun it was this way,

Melanie," Shane cut in, leaning closer to me. "Imagine Doc Ellis's eyes bugging out as he sits in his rented room, smoking cigarettes and grading perfect test after perfect test—"

"Rented room?"

"Yeah, I imagine him living in this rented room, so he can pretend he's still in a dorm or whatever."

I hid my smile behind my hand.

Shane still looked dreamy. "Anyway, can't you just see him, settling down for a happy session of feeling superior to us and then slowly realizing—"

"Realizing that we cheated and flunking us all," I said shortly.

"Come on," Shane coaxed. "It's already over and done with. Let's at least have a little fun—"

"Watching all my hard work go down the drain?" I snapped.

Shane shook his head, still smiling faintly. "I can see I'm not going to get through to you." Then a flash of worry crossed his face. "Hey, you're not going to tell your dad about this, are you?"

I nearly went up in smoke. "Is that where all this let's-be-friends business is coming from?" Anger made my throat tight, and the words came out in a whisper. "To make sure I wouldn't rat on you?"

"No, it just occurred to me—"

"Just occurred to you that I automatically tell my father everything?" I demanded. "I'm not a snitch, Shane, and I don't need you to remind me to keep my mouth shut."

"Melanie—"

"Furthermore," I continued, "the reason I won't tell is because I never tell. I've been in this situation a million times and never told. It has nothing to do with you. If there's a person it would give me more pleasure to see get in trouble, I don't know who it is."

Shane took my outburst very calmly—much more so than I'd have liked. He looked thoughtful. "What about Mrs. McCracken?" he said finally.

"What?"

"You said that if there were a person it would give you more pleasure to see get in trouble than me, you didn't know who it was and I said—"

"I *heard* what you said!"

"Relax," he said softly. "You look like you're going to have a heart attack. You really need to learn to get more fun out of life." He began walking away from me toward the cafeteria. I could see his shoulders shaking with laughter.

"There's more to life than fun!" I called after him. "Fun isn't—" I broke off suddenly, imagining how I must sound.

I felt like some evil elf, some miserly gnome, declaring *There will be no such thing as fun.* And I wasn't like that, not normally. Shane just made me feel so—so severe. Of course, other kids made me feel that way sometimes too—take Marty Richards and his it's-past-your-bedtime comments, for instance. But somehow I could just shrug Marty off. Shane was a different story. Shane drove me crazy.

After school I grabbed my Taco Bell uniform out of my locker and headed to the bathroom to change. I won't go into very much detail about my Taco Bell job. Suffice it to say that one of my major career objectives is to find a job someday that doesn't require me to wear this particular shade of Taco Bell brown.

To make matters worse, our Taco Bell management has instituted a new policy: all employees must appear on the job already dressed in their uniforms. This brilliant new policy was established in the name of morale and efficiency; the management seems to think that if we arrive at work in uniform, we'll have instant Taco Bell spirit and will have to spend less time making the transition to work mode. Fortunately the policy is just an experiment. I'm hoping that in a couple of weeks the management will realize that making us dress up for work any sooner than we absolutely have to isn't exactly going to boost our Taco Bell spirit.

As I changed into my uniform I considered suggesting that Taco Bell sponsor some sort of beauty contest, with girls from all over the country modeling Taco Bell uniforms. They could offer some outrageous prize, like a million dollars, to the girl who actually managed to look attractive in one. The company would get tons of publicity and at the same time they could be perfectly confident that they wouldn't have to award the prize. A supermodel wouldn't look pretty in Taco Bell brown.

I finished changing and was just about to swing open the bathroom door when I heard the soft sound of boys' laughter outside. Now, I know that sooner or later *some* boy is going to spot me walking down the school hallway wearing my uniform, but I was determined to keep exposure to a minimum. I stood at the bathroom door and waited for the laughter to fade.

But the boys didn't seem to be moving on.

"So do you think this will work?" a boy asked. It sounded as though he were right outside the door.

"Trust me. We switched bathroom signs in my old school, and it was great. I mean, I hate to rehash the same old prank, but this one's worth rehashing. It's amazing the way people freak out when they realize they're in the wrong place. Especially this certain brand of innocent girl, you know?"

My heart started to hammer. I was pretty sure that the first boy who spoke was Marty Richards, but I had no question about the second one.

Shane Conner, getting all psyched to witness someone's humiliation. And I could think of one person Shane would categorize as a "certain brand of innocent girl." Me.

From the sound of things, the boys had brought a bazillion supplies and were going to work on the bathroom door. I pictured myself having to spend the night in the girls'-turned-boys' room as I waited for the guys to leave.

"So are you going to have a party this weekend?" By now I was sure the boy with Shane was Marty.

"I don't know yet," Shane replied.

"I thought you said your parents were going to be out of town."

"They are," Shane said patiently. "But I'm not sure I want to have a party just yet."

"Why not?"

"Well, because I don't know all that many people," Shane explained. "And I don't want things to get out of control."

"They won't," Marty said. I wondered what Marty thought he was talking about. Was he promising that everyone who came to Shane's party would behave themselves? Good luck.

"Besides," Shane continued, "my parents would kill me if they found out."

"How would they find out?"

"Well, if, like, something really valuable got broken," Shane said reasonably. "Plus I live right across the street from Merrill, if you can believe it."

"Oh, he's a pretty good guy," Marty said. "I don't think he'd rat on you."

I grinned. Thank you, Marty Richards! I loved it when kids at school, especially popular kids, weren't too cool to admit that my dad was a decent guy, even if he was the principal.

"Maybe," Shane said. "But Melanie's another story. I mean, with her there it's, like, constant supervision."

It seemed to me that the planet turned very slowly in the next moment. Shane's sentence repeated itself in my mind about twenty times in the space of two heartbeats. I felt completely numb. *Please defend me,* I begged Marty silently. *Tell Shane he doesn't know what he's talking about—that as much as you tease me, I'm not just some goody-goody principal's daughter. That I'm actually pretty cool.*

"Yeah, I guess she's not the biggest partyer in the world," Marty remarked.

I felt myself flush. Not the biggest partyer in the world? Well, no, maybe I wasn't exactly known for throwing parties where all the windows were shattering from the noise, but lots of kids weren't, and *they* didn't get stereotyped as boring, straightlaced goody-goodies. I couldn't believe it. Marty calls my father a pretty good guy, but thinks I'd—I'd call the cops because my neighbor threw a party? I sounded like someone's grandmother.

"She's got a good case of principal's daughter syndrome, if you ask me," Shane continued. "It's too bad because she's . . . well, she's . . . I don't know, she's kind of . . ."

"She's *what*, Conner?" Marty asked impatiently.

Shane cleared his throat. "Well, she's way critical. I'll bet she was the only person in Doc Ellis's class today who didn't appreciate my, um, humble effort with the answer sheet."

My heart was now beating so violently I was almost sure they'd hear it through the door. Did he honestly think I was the *only* person? Did he think I was nothing but the school's resident drip? And why did I care what he thought of me, anyway? My only wish right now was that somehow he and Marty would both disappear so that I could make a mad dash for Taco Bell.

"Gentlemen? What exactly are you doing to the bathroom door?"

I could have sobbed with relief. Mrs. McCracken to the rescue! I never thought I'd be so glad to hear her drone.

"Oh, um, hi, Mrs. McCracken," Marty stammered. "We were just, um—"

"We were giving this sign here a good polish," Shane filled in quickly. "I always think it's a shame when the school facilities aren't in the condition they could be. We just wanted to do our part. Well, now that that's taken care of, I guess we should be on our way. . . ."

Mrs. McCracken clucked her tongue. There was a shuffle of feet and some mumbled conversation, and finally I was alone again. But I didn't run out of the bathroom right away. Instead I stood, red faced, in front of the mirror. *A good case of principal's daughter syndrome,* I repeated to myself. *Way critical.* I knew that I wasn't exactly beautiful in my Taco Bell uniform, but Shane's words made me feel plainer than ever.

After work that night I'd managed to calm down. I was not, repeat not, going to let Shane Conner's opinion have such a strong effect on me. I'd made it home from my short shift in time for dessert.

I was helping myself to some salad my mother had put aside for me when the phone rang. I had a psychic flash that it was going to be Doc Ellis and my heart beat a little faster.

My father talked for a few minutes and then came back to the dinner table and sat down. He picked up his fork and said thoughtfully, "That was Ladd Ellis."

I almost laughed in spite of my thudding heart. I mean, Ladd? It's always hilarious to hear teachers call each other by their first names, even when they have *normal* first names.

My father was looking at me strangely. "Are you okay, Melanie?"

"Yes, indeed," I said, taking a drink of milk.

"How is Ladd?" my mother said cheerfully. She is not very adept at picking up nuances. You could come into the room white as a ghost and say, *The morgue just called,* and my mother would say *Really? How are things at the morgue?*

My father was still staring at me. "He said that he had just discovered something curious. He was grading the tests he gave today and he noticed that Bobby Weller got a hundred."

"Good for Bobby," my mother said, missing the point entirely.

My father gave *her* a look now. "So, anyway," he said slowly. "Ladd went back and looked at the other tests and realized that *everyone* had gotten perfect scores."

I couldn't hold my laughter in this time. Imagine Doc Ellis grading perfect test after perfect test and only realizing something was amiss when Bobby Weller got a good grade! I snorted milk back into my glass.

"Gross," said Joy, watching.

"Sorry," I said, still smiling.

"Oh," said my mother, getting it at last. "It sounds like organized cheating on a grand scale."

My father sighed. "Ladd said he hadn't graded your test yet, Melanie, but I don't suppose it matters. He can't count these scores anyway."

"Why not?" said Joy. "Maybe it was an easy test or a coincidence or something."

"Coincidence?" Pride said scornfully. "Do

you know what the odds are against that?"

Joy shrugged. "No," she said wearily.

"I could do the problem in my head if I knew all the details," Pride went on. She's very talented at math. "How many students are there and how many questions on the test?" she asked me.

"You don't really care," Joy told her. "You just want to show off. It's just like Ms. Gregson says—"

"Girls," my father. "This isn't the time—"

"Joy, what exactly did Ms. Gregson say?" my mother said.

"That Pride *shows off*," Joy said happily. "That she doesn't *encourage others who need more time*, that she—"

"Much more time," Pride murmured darkly, looking daggers at Joy.

"Sweetheart," my mother said, "you know that we're very proud of your math skills, but—"

"Bah!" shouted Charity from her high chair.

"Girls," my father said again. "Listen—"

"You *are* a total show-off, Pride," I said quickly before my father could continue. I didn't want to talk about Doc Ellis's test anymore, and if there's one thing I've learned over the years, it's that I can usually shut my dad out of a conversation by squabbling with my sisters.

He sat back, defeated, with a look on his face that said: Are all fathers with four daughters bullied like this?

* * *

"Just a minute, Mel. I want to ask you something," my father said later that night when I walked into the kitchen to get a snack. He was bathing Charity in the sink.

"Mah!" Charity shouted, laughing. She splashed water everywhere when she saw me.

"Hi, Charity bunny," I said, leaning over to kiss the top of her soapy head.

"Gah!" she shouted. She hasn't said her first word yet, but my mother says it should happen any day now.

I took an apple from the basket on the counter as I waited for my father to say whatever was on his mind.

My father picked up Charity, stood her on the counter, and began rubbing her dry with a pink towel.

"Rah!" she yelled happily. She likes to be dried off.

"Mel," my father said again. "I don't suppose you know anything about Doc Ellis's test that you want to tell me?"

I took a bite of my apple. "No," I said carefully.

My father and I struck a deal a long time ago. He never asks any direct questions about incidents at school; he just asks if there's anything I want to tell him. I'm free to say yes or no and we leave it at that.

He sighed. "I didn't think so."

He kept rubbing Charity, wrapping her completely in the pink towel. I watched the two of them in the yellow glow of the kitchen light. My father looked tired, but his hands touched Charity with infinite patience, as though he had nothing better to do than keep drying an already dry baby.

"Sorry about the test," he said at last. "I know how hard you studied."

Which shows you the kind of absolute faith my father has in me. I stepped closer and put my arms around him from behind. Across the street I could see a shadow moving around and wondered if it was Shane. Could he see the three of us, enclosed in the glow of the kitchen lamp?

Then I shook my head, determined to banish all thoughts of Shane Conner.

FOUR

SATURDAY MORNING I stood by the back door in my nightgown, saying, "Yes, Mom . . . yes, I'll eat up the meatballs . . . yes, I'll take out the trash . . . no, I'm not going to have a party. . . ."

My parents were taking my sisters on a weekend color tour of northern Michigan. I didn't have to go with them because I get carsick very easily.

And if I didn't get carsick easily, I would fake it because there is nothing more boring than driving around in a car and commenting on red or gold leaves. I'm surprised that Pride and Joy aren't smart enough to object yet. Actually I think they play Battleship pretty much constantly throughout the trip.

My mother shifted Charity to her other hip. "And don't make any long-distance phone calls," she said finally.

"Mom, who would I call?"

"Oh, I don't know . . ." My mother smiled. "I guess I was just struggling for some final word of advice."

"Believe me, I think you've covered everything."

My father honked the horn. He was the only one sitting in the car. Pride and Joy were standing by the open back hatch, arguing about who had to ride in the "way back" of the station wagon. If I could give my father one word of wisdom, it would be: You can't make a female get in the car before she's ready to get in the car. Actually I have conveyed this bit of wisdom, but he doesn't seem to believe it.

"Good-bye, sweetie," my mother said. She kissed my cheek and went out to the car.

I closed the door with a happy sigh. I had the house to myself for twenty-four hours. Katie was coming over soon to spend the day and night here. We would have the whole weekend to talk and sleep in and eat junk food and all that stuff that parents are always disapproving of.

I decided to surprise Katie and make pancakes for brunch. I mixed the batter and heated the griddle. The first pancakes turned out burned and mottled, so I threw them into the wastebasket. I was just making a big pancake in the shape of Mickey Mouse's head when the doorbell rang.

I galloped through the house and threw open the door.

"Hurry up and come in," I said, "because I'm making pancakes and I don't—"

I stopped, horrified. It wasn't Katie standing on the front porch. It was Shane Conner.

He smiled lazily. "Can I borrow a cup of Liquid-Plumr?"

I crossed my arms. "Funny joke. Good-bye."

"Hey," Shane protested. "It's not a joke; our tub is about an inch from overflowing and my parents are gone in the car and—do you think I made this up just to see you in your exceptionally short nightgown?"

I blushed to the roots of my hair. I was wearing this silly coffee-colored satin baby doll nightgown that my grandmother gave me. She gives me one every Christmas and birthday. I don't know exactly what she's trying to tell me. Anyway, this particular one was not only short to begin with, it also was a couple of years old and a little too small for me.

I pressed my hands against the ridiculously short hem in case a gust of wind should happen along and said icily, "There are plenty of other houses on this street. Go ask someone who doesn't actively hate—"

The smoke alarm buzzed angrily in the kitchen. I broke off and sprinted back through the house. The kitchen was foggy with smoke and my Mickey Mouse pancake was a charred mess. I turned off the griddle and struggled to open a window.

"Hey," said a voice behind me. "Should we have wet washcloths over our mouths? Where's the baking soda?"

I spun around. Shane was standing right there in the kitchen. I waved some smoke out of the air in front of my face and glared at him. "What are you doing in here?"

"I have to borrow some Liquid-Plumr," he said patiently. "I think we just covered that."

"And I said you *couldn't,*" I snapped. The smoke alarm went off again and I reached up on tiptoe and pressed the switch.

Shane laughed. "I see London, I see France—"

"Shut up!" I shouted. I dropped my arms and opened a kitchen drawer. I tied on my father's barbecue apron. Luckily it was so big it wrapped all the way around me twice.

Shane smiled. "Now you look like the fantasy I used to have about this really beautiful home-ec teacher at my old school."

I pointed the spatula at him. "Shut up about your fantasies." I grabbed the bottle of Drano from under the sink and handed it to him. "You have two seconds to get out of here."

He leaned against the counter. He was wearing a salmon-colored sweatshirt that looked so old I suspected it had probably been red at one time. The rosy color brightened his smooth brown face, and his clear eyes twinkled. For no reason at all I remembered the way his hand had felt when he put it on my waist at Bobby Weller's party. He looked so crisp and clean that I felt even frumpier and more exposed in my nightgown.

"So where's your family?" Shane asked.

"Out of town," I said automatically. "I thought your tub was overflowing."

"It will if one more drop of water falls into it. Out of town, huh?" he said, moving to stand next to me. "And I can see you're really letting your hair down, making pancakes in the shape of Mickey Mouse. Very brazen. What exciting thing do have planned for tonight? An omelette in the shape of Daffy Duck?"

I gave him a withering look.

He smiled back. "Well, good luck with the pancake," he said conversationally.

I thought of how happy I'd been only ten minutes ago at the prospect of my lazy weekend. And now he'd come in here basically telling me for the millionth time what a dull priss I was.

"Good-bye," I said loudly.

"I'm going, I'm going," he said. "The excitement in here is too much for me anyway."

I followed him through the living room, still armed with the spatula. He lingered in the doorway. "I guess it would be too much to expect you to have a party," he said mockingly. "After all, you are the principal's daughter and such a good little girl—hey—"

I pushed him bodily out the door. He stumbled out onto the porch and I slammed the heavy door shut behind him.

I turned and caught sight of myself in the hall mirror. I was the picture of fury: chalky skin, flashing eyes, lips tightened, chest heaving, brow perspiring.

Well, naturally I would look furious. I *was* furious. But somehow, as mad as I felt, I couldn't help wishing that I'd looked prettier while Shane was here.

Katie was hours late getting to my house and when she did, bad news was written all over her small face.

"What happened?" I asked, taking her jacket.

Katie threw herself onto the couch. She sighed deeply. "You won't believe who asked me to the Fall Ball."

"Who?"

"Guess," she said dramatically. "Just guess. Think of the last person you would ever want to *know* your phone number, much less call you up and ask you out."

I thought for a second. "Highwater Pat?"

Katie groaned and threw her overnight bag on the floor.

"Yes," she shouted. "Yes! Yes! Yes!"

I started laughing. "You mean I guessed? I actually guessed?"

Katie threw me a murderous look. "What's so funny?"

I put on a straight face. "I'm sorry, Katie. I just didn't think Pat was actually the guy you meant."

Highwater Pat *is* most girls' absolute last choice for a date. I don't feel great saying that, because he's not a *bad* guy exactly. I mean, there are certainly guys at school who are creepier. There's nothing all that remarkable about Highwater Pat's looks—he's kind of chubby, with curly brown hair—except for maybe his cheeks, which are extremely pink. Then, of course, there's the fact that he always wears pants that are too short for him. You would think that after kids started calling him "Highwater Pat" he would get the message and stop wearing them, but no. I try not to call him by his nickname, but since everyone else calls him "Highwater Pat," it's easy to slip and forget.

But I think the thing that really dooms Pat to unpopularity is his overeager, superfriendly personality. He's *so* friendly, in fact, that if you're a reasonably nice person to begin with, you feel bad just ignoring him or walking away even when he's annoying you to death.

Katie sighed again, so heavily that I had a brief vision of her emptying her lungs completely and losing consciousness. "What am I going to do?"

"What do you mean?" I asked. "Didn't you say no?"

"Of course I said no!" Katie sobbed.

"Katie, Katie," I said soothingly, in the same voice you would use to a madman with a gun. "I know it's really awkward rejecting someone's invitation to the Fall Ball, but really, it's going to be okay."

"No, it's not!" Katie leapt off the couch and grabbed my shoulders. Her words were hushed and rapid, as though she were imparting vital information. "My mother says that I have to go with the first boy who asks me or I can't go at all. She thinks this whole business of rejecting creates a damaging, exclusive atmosphere and that I shouldn't take the Fall Ball so seriously anyway."

"Oh, no." I covered my mouth in horror. "So it's Highwater Pat or no one?"

"Will you *quit* saying his name every few seconds?" Katie was still whispering furiously at me. "My mother wouldn't even know that High— that *he* had asked me except that she answered the phone and he asked her permission!"

"He *what*?"

"You heard me."

"Sheesh," I muttered. "What did he think he was doing, proposing?"

"I know!" Katie moaned. "Just tell me what I'm going to do."

I rubbed her shoulder sympathetically. She sat up and grabbed a tissue out of a box on the coffee table. She blew her nose and looked out the window. Dusk had fallen, and the windows of the Conners' house were warmly lit. Cars were already lined up along both sides of the street.

"Hey," Katie said softly. "Shane's having a party."

Katie peered through my mother's bird-watching binoculars. "They just brought out another keg," she announced.

It was midnight, and the party at Shane's was rocking so loudly that I doubt anyone in a ten-mile radius could sleep. Katie and I sat at my bedroom window, pajama clad, watching. That sounds more pathetic than it actually was. You have to realize that the party was so loud that we couldn't watch TV, we couldn't listen to the radio, we couldn't talk on the phone. We could barely hear each other! I took some cold comfort in the fact that probably everyone attending the party would suffer permanent hearing loss.

Katie was being a very good sport. When I told her the excruciating story about overhearing Shane in the boys' bathroom, she said immediately that she wouldn't dream of going to any party thrown by that jerk. But now I could see how her eyes sparkled as she watched the other partygoers. Poor Katie, I thought. She can't go to the biggest party of the year because she's best friends with the mealymouthed principal's daughter.

I wouldn't have thought it possible, but the music

coming from Shane's house suddenly jumped another decibel level. I could feel the rhythm pounding in my sternum. I actually felt a little queasy.

Cars were double and triple parked along the street as far as the eye could see. I think I probably saw more cars that night than I had all year. Silhouettes filled every window of the Connor house. Every time someone moved out of sight, five new people moved to take his or her place. The stream of people in the front door was continuous. Shane stood at the front door—

I grabbed the binoculars from Katie and peered through them. "He's taking money from people!" I shouted. "He's charging admission. He's probably going to turn a profit!"

Katie looked at me, puzzled, and I realized suddenly that she hadn't been able to hear a word I said. I cupped my hands against her ear and started repeating myself, but she gestured impatiently and pointed to the street.

A police cruiser was threading its way through the parked cars. It pulled to a stop in front of the Conners' house, and a cop hopped out and went stomping across the lawn.

The music shut off immediately. The policeman stood on the porch with Shane, gesturing sternly.

"I wonder if Shane can hear anything he's saying," Katie said. "Or if his eardrums burst, like, an hour ago."

"He's probably just nodding at what he suspects are the right moments," I agreed.

We watched for a few minutes as people surged out of the house and tried to find their cars in the street. It looked like a human river.

"Finally we can sleep," Katie said, dropping onto one of the twin beds in my room. "Good night." She threw her arm over her eyes and was asleep in two seconds. I lingered at the window, watching as the last people left.

Shane stood on the porch, a policeman at his side, nodding graciously to everyone. When the last person left, he shook hands with the policeman and then watched until the cruiser pulled away from the curb and drove off down the street.

Shane leaned against one of the columns on the porch. I could see his silhouette perfectly in the light that blazed from every window. I wondered why he wasn't running around, picking up beer bottles and trying to restore his parents' house to something resembling normalcy. He didn't seem like a kid throwing a party. He seemed like an adult, a grown-up, someone with no worries. Grudgingly I admired his cool as I watched him stand on his front porch, inhaling the cool night air.

After a while he straightened up and stretched. Then he waved at my window.

For a moment I felt a hot flush of embarrassment. Had he known I was watching the whole time? *With Melanie there, it's like constant supervision,* I could hear him saying to Marty. What if he thought I was the one who had called the cops?

But as he gave me a final wave, I felt somehow that for once he wasn't making fun of me. It was as though we shared a secret, though what that was I couldn't say.

FIVE

FOR A COUPLE of days after the great cheating episode, Doc Ellis looked so crumpled and defeated that I actually felt a little sorry for him. But then he seemed to recover his former acidic humor and threw himself into creating a diabolically difficult new math test.

Now he stood at the front of the classroom. "I have graded your papers," he said wearily. "I think that most of you—dare I say all of you?—will find that you fared less well on the New Improved Test than you did on the old model."

He began wandering up and down the aisle, distributing papers and making snide comments: "Quite a tumble, Debra . . . Mitchell, I'm amazed that you had such a grasp on the material just last week. . . . Sorry to disappoint you, Melanie."

He dropped my test faceup on my desk. None of that coy, anonymous, facedown stuff for Doc Ellis. I looked at the grade: seventy-one. It figured. No amount of studying could have prepared me for the wretchedly hard New Improved Test.

The bell rang. I gathered my things and headed toward my next class. Shane fell in step beside me.

"What'd you get on the test?" he asked cheerily.

I stared straight ahead. It was his fault there was a New Improved Test in the first place, and I wasn't about to disguise my anger. "Seventy-one," I said coldly.

"Oh, I got a sixty-four," he said. "I changed one of my answers so many times, there was actually a hole in the paper."

I gave him a chilly smile. "Sorry I'm not more sympathetic."

"That's okay," he said, ignoring my sarcasm. He kept walking beside me, and since he was in my next class, beginning drama, I imagined he intended to walk with me all the way there.

We walked in silence for a minute, and then as we passed the guidance center Shane touched my elbow. "Wait just a minute," he said lightly. "I want to look at the ride board."

I paused, curious. Shane didn't seem like the kind of person who'd make use of the college ride board, which is basically a bulletin announcing visits to various colleges. Anyone who's going to visit a college is supposed to put up a notice so that other people can go with them and save on gas and cut down on pollution and generally escape from their parents for a day or so. My father is inordinately proud of the college ride board even though it never works. I guess most parents are entirely too uptight and want to go along and see the colleges for themselves.

"Do you think a lot of people will be signing up for these visits?" Shane asked with a snicker. I looked over his shoulder at the notices he was reading. They were all for places like the American University in Beirut and Cambridge University and the New School of Economics in Delhi. In the space provided for "Gas/Other Expenses" people had written "$2,800 airfare" and under "Estimated Travel Time" they'd written "356 hours."

I shook my head. My father was going to be crushed. "Did you have something to do with this?" I asked suspiciously.

"Me?" he asked innocently.

"You know, the college ride board means a lot to my father," I told him.

"I can see why," Shane said. "It's very useful."

I narrowed my eyes. "What about rewiring the attendance bell to play 'Shave and a Haircut' last week?" I asked. "My father had to hire a special electrician to come in and rewire it."

Shane nodded solemnly. "It's a good thing too. It's hard to take your studies seriously when the attendance bell plays a song like that."

"Oh, give me a break!" I exclaimed, furious on my father's behalf. "Don't even try to pretend you weren't—"

"What about the betting pool on Mrs. McCracken's age?" Shane broke in, smiling brightly.

I blinked. "So that *was* you!"

"Well, I didn't say that exactly . . ."

I rolled my eyes and flounced ahead of him down the hall and into beginning drama. Beginning drama was actually one of my favorite classes. The teacher, Mr. Munger, is this gentle soul who encourages everyone, regardless of acting ability, and never scolds or lectures. Plus we didn't have tests.

"Hello, everyone," Mr. Munger said in a hoarse voice when we were all seated. "I have a sore throat, so all I want you to do is sit tight and read *Twelve Angry Men*." He shrugged. "Or do homework for your other classes, or talk among yourselves or whatever."

He sat at his desk and began reading a *Batman* comic book. I was just beginning my math homework when there was a knock at the door.

Mr. Munger pointed at Jubilee Smith. "What?" she asked.

"Say 'Come in,'" Mr. Munger commanded hoarsely.

Jubilee cleared her throat like someone auditioning for a play and said, "Come in!" in this stupid dramatic way.

The door opened and a big beefy guy dragging a trolley came in. He had a clipboard. "Salvation Army," he announced. "Here to pick up the cotton candy machine."

Now it so happens that Knox High does have a cotton candy machine. Or rather, Mr. Munger does. He's always making cotton candy during his free hour.

Mr. Munger looked surprised. "I'm afraid there's been a mistake," he said huskily. "I don't have a candy machine."

The Salvation Army guy looked at the cotton candy machine in the corner.

Mr. Munger smiled wryly. "Well, I don't have one that I want to give away," he amended.

The Salvation Army guy looked really fed up. "Listen, fella, I got the call, I came all the way out here."

Mr. Munger raised his eyebrows. "I didn't make the call."

The Salvation Army guy seemed to think that over. "Well, someone made a call."

I shot a glance at Shane. He beamed proudly.

"Listen, it doesn't matter who called," the Salvation Army man said. "The point is, I came all the way out here. What are you doing with the machine, anyway? Is a school anyplace for that?"

I wanted to defend Mr. Munger. I mean, so maybe making cotton candy in your free period isn't completely normal and maybe it doesn't further the cause of higher education, but who was it hurting?

Certainly not Shane, who obviously just loved causing trouble for the sake of it.

The burly Salvation Army guy leaned over Mr. Munger. "Wouldn't you rather a lot of poor children had that candy?"

Mr. Munger looked perplexed. "Well, I guess . . ." Suddenly he perked up, seemingly swept away by the community spirit. "Go ahead, take it!" he said grandly. "Give it to needy children. I'm happy to donate it!"

I sighed. I guess donating a cotton candy machine to the Salvation Army is an okay idea in the scheme of things, but I couldn't help thinking Mr. Munger would miss his machine when fifth hour rolled around. I looked once more at Shane, who was working on his German homework with studied casualness.

"Well, everyone, the big day has arrived," Smiler said later that afternoon, smiling at us madly.

Smiler is the biology teacher, and the big day to which he was referring was our first day in the lab dissecting things. Of course, in Smiler's opinion the *really* big day would be when we got to chapter eight (reproduction). Smiler lives to teach sex ed. On the first day of class he beamed at us and said, "I know you're all looking forward to chapter eight as much as I am, but we're just going to have to wait." He's pretty much insane. He has this crazy grin on his face all the time, which is why everyone, even my father, calls him Smiler. He's basically some kind of pervert, but his perversion is well cloaked in academic language, and I guess the school can't fire him just for talking a whole lot about stamens and pistils and sperm and ova.

Smiler shuffled a big sheaf of papers and beamed at us. "I have assigned all of you lab partners," he said.

This was greeted by a general chorus of groans. Everyone knows that Smiler wants every pair of lab partners to consist of a boy and a girl so he can watch their every move and see if they fall in love or kiss or whatever it is he's waiting for.

I knows that sounds bizarre, but it's the truth. On the first day of class Smiler had said, "Why don't you all just mingle amongst yourselves and tomorrow I'll come up with a seating chart?" So everyone had to sit around talking while Smiler watched us like a hawk. The next day he came running in with this seating chart that had everyone arranged in—surprise!—boy-girl pairs. He made no secret of the fact that he did this as some sort of matchmaking endeavor.

So on the second day of school I found myself sitting next to Teddy Inman. Teddy Inman is this senior who's been held back about two or three times and, if possible, he's an even bigger pervert than Smiler himself. Last year he got suspended for bringing copies of *Playboy* to school and selling individual pages to freshmen for fifty cents apiece. Plus he's just fairly creepy in general and wears this leather jacket and sort of slouches and sneers all the time. Now, imagine Smiler mulling it over and thinking, *Hmmm, I guess I'll put Melanie with Teddy. . . . Maybe they'll hit it off!* I have to say, it didn't make me feel too good about the image I was projecting.

"Okay, now, everyone listen up: here are your partners," Smiler told us in a booming voice. "Brad Hopkins, Candace Miller."

Brad and Candace exchanged grateful looks. They've been friends forever.

"Jubilee Smith and Bobby Weller."

Jubilee shot Smiler a murderous look. I would've too. Can you imagine having the school's slacker as your lab partner? Bobby looked vaguely startled to have his name called at all.

"Swiss Kriss and Teddy Inman," Smiler continued.

Teddy cast a creepy look at Swiss Kriss, who looked perceptibly terrified. I didn't blame her. It was probably only a matter of time before Teddy did something vile, like put his hand on her leg.

Smiler preceded to pair up the rest of the class. Finally, he looked right at me, a gleam in his eye.

"And last but not least, Melanie Merrill and Shane Conner," he said briskly, and set down the folder. "Now, let's all go to the lab to start dissecting those worms!"

I walked numbly to the lab, staring straight ahead. I'd been so interested in everyone else's partner that I hadn't stopped to consider my own. So I was stuck with Shane. At that moment Teddy Inman and Bobby Weller seemed like really appealing lab partners.

Shane bounced up to me. "Well, isn't this a happy coincidence?" he said cheerily. "Or is it a coincidence? Perhaps you used your family influence to bribe Smiler and ensure getting me as your partner."

I held the scalpel from my lab kit against his throat. "Listen," I said through gritted teeth. "I'm only going to be your lab partner if you keep your odious comments to yourself and if you do all the gross stuff."

He looked thoughtful. "Define *gross*."

I removed the scalpel. He didn't seem threatened by it anyway. "Touching the worms with your hands, even if you're wearing gloves. Same goes for the frogs and pigs when we get to them. Cutting the worms or frogs and especially the pigs open. Wiping up any blood that spills. Touching anything that might once have been something's brain."

He frowned. "So what exactly do you do?"

I snapped the surgical tweezers at him. "I'll dig around inside once you've done the dirty work and identify organs and stuff."

"Okay," he said. "It's a deal." His eyes sparkled. "But as for keeping my odious comments to myself, I'm sorry, but that's asking just a little too much."

I rolled my eyes. "Figures," I muttered under my breath.

We opened the box with the worm in it. I recoiled from the formaldehyde smell. The worm lay stiff and rubbery on the bottom.

"Oh," I said, relieved. "It's dead."

"Well, of course it is." Shane laughed. "What did you think, we were going to have to club it over the head first?"

I blushed. "Well, no—"

"Good to see you two getting along," Smiler said, coming up behind us. That's another thing about Smiler—you practically never get in trouble for talking in his class because he always thinks you're flirting, which he approves of. He gave us a big goofy smile and moved on.

"Sheesh," Shane said, pulling on a pair of plastic gloves.

"There is something seriously wrong with that guy."

"I know."

We worked on the worm in silence for a few

minutes. It wasn't really that gross. The worm had probably been soaking in formaldehyde for about twenty years and was so stretchy and fake feeling that it didn't even seem like a real animal—or a real invertebrate, as the case may be.

Working with Shane wasn't as bad as I thought it would be either. He was pretty conscientious, taking careful notes and even labeling my drawing while I dictated the names to him. I was certainly doing better than Jubilee, who was next to us, carping at Bobby Weller. Bobby seemed mesmerized by the motion of the agitator, which was dissolving copper sulfate for the fifth-hour chem class. His mouth was hanging open a little bit.

"Hey, hey, hey," Shane said mildly. "You just squashed its brain. I thought you weren't going to have anything to do with brains."

"That's its brain?" I squinted dubiously at the end of the tweezers. "How can you tell? It's so small."

"Well, I don't think worms have all that many thoughts," Shane said. "But then, neither would you if all you did was tunnel through dirt all day."

We both examined the mashed worm brain sticking to my tweezers. I suddenly realized that I had never stood so close to Shane before. It gave me an odd feeling, like when you see a celebrity in person. We were the same height, and I could see that his thick brown lashes were golden on the ends. His skin was really clear—no small feat for someone in high school—and almost olive. I noticed for the first time that he had high cheekbones. I knew that any girl would have died for those cheekbones; I wondered if he had any sisters and if they had cheekbones like that. But I couldn't picture anyone in Shane's family. His looks seemed so unique, so much *him,* that I couldn't imagine anyone who shared his features.

I noticed Shane's piercing green eyes were examining me with a watchful expression that I couldn't quite recognize.

"Hey, Smiler?" he said softly, still looking at me.

"Yes?" Smiler said immediately. I hadn't even realized he was standing next to us.

"Melanie has something she wants to say to you," Shane said. Still he was standing so close to me, still staring.

"What's that?" Smiler asked.

"She wants to say . . ." Shane dropped his eyes and stepped away from me. He busied himself with the lab kit. "She wants to say that she's really happy you put us together as lab partners."

I gasped. How dare he embarrass me!

"Delighted to hear it," Smiler said radiantly. He wiggled his bushy eyebrows at me.

SIX

I WAS CRAMMING for a Spanish test during lunch the next day when I heard a familiar voice ask with mock courtesy, "Is this seat taken?"

I knew it was Shane even before I looked up. I'd seen him earlier sitting at Alex Chase and Marty Richards's table, which happens to be the most popular table in the cafeteria. Just thinking about it, I felt a familiar flicker of jealousy; Shane had a *crowd*.

"Yes," I said.

He sat down anyway across from me at the space Katie had vacated five minutes before. He looked at Katie's tray. "I guess I should say, Is this lunch taken? Wow, a hamburger. I had the chili." He picked up her burger and took a bite.

I cringed. "That is so gross. You don't even

know whose food that is or why they abandoned it."

"True . . ." He was still chewing. "It's pretty good, though." He looked at me. "Do you think waiters eat the leftover food off your plate when they take it back to the kitchen?"

"I never thought about it," I said coolly, suddenly sure that I would think of nothing else every time I ate out.

"And furthermore," Shane continued in between bites of Katie's hamburger. "What if they really like what you're eating and are hoping for some scraps and then you ask for a doggie bag?"

I just shook my head in response as I watched him polishing off Katie's lunch. "How can you eat that?" I asked. "I hate school hamburgers."

"Yeah, well, you should have gone to my old school," Shane said. "Do you want to hear the story about how this new kid ate the pizza and got really sick and nobody could figure it out because a lot of people had eaten slices from the very same pizza and none of them had gotten sick?"

"He had the flu?" I guessed.

"No, it turns out that there was something—some bacteria—in the food and we were all immune to it because we'd been eating it unknowingly for so many years, but the new kid wasn't immune and you should have seen—"

I looked Shane straight in the eye. "That story does not have one single redeeming feature."

Shane looked absurdly pleased, like I'd just

paid him a huge compliment. "I know," he said, unconcerned. "Listen, I want to ask you something."

"No, I didn't call the police the night of your party," I said. I turned a page of my Spanish book.

"That wasn't my question," Shane said. "I know you didn't call the police. It was Mrs. Hewlett. I know because she also called my parents. Why would I think it was you?"

I looked at him stonily. All at once his conversation with Marty rushed back to me with amazing clarity. *With Melanie there, it's like constant supervision. . . . She's got a case of principal's daughter syndrome.* The memory made my face burn.

Shane was looking at me intently, a small flicker of something deep in his eyes. "Melanie?" he said softly. "What's up?"

I shook my head. I was not about to give him the satisfaction of knowing I'd heard that humiliating conversation. "Nothing."

He shrugged. "Well, what I wanted to ask you," he said slowly, now eating Katie's brownie, "is if you want to be vice president of this club I'm starting."

I narrowed my eyes. "What kind of club? Is it school sponsored?"

He looked interested. "What do you mean?"

"I mean, does a teacher or someone, you

know, *sponsor* it, like a coach or whatever."

Shane frowned. "I didn't know I needed that."

"You do if you want to put it on college applications," I said. "What kind of club did you say it was?"

"I don't know yet."

"What's the name of it?"

"I haven't picked one."

"Well, what's the club going to *do*?" I asked, exasperated.

He waved his hand dismissively. "I guess not all that much, although I think it might be nice to have some sort of fund-raiser and then take the money and throw a party."

"Who is going to give money to a bunch of kids to throw a party?" I asked.

"Well, obviously I'm not going to tell anyone what we're raising funds *for*," Shane said patiently. "But I don't think anyone's going to ask, do you? I mean, when you buy stuff at a bake sale or whatever, do you quiz the person selling it to you?"

"No, but—"

"That's why the club needs a really good name," Shane said. "Do you, as vice president, have any suggestions?"

"Look," I said, standing up and gathering my books, "I am not going to be the vice president of any club that's so dishonest and unscrupulous."

"Hey," Shane said mildly. "I didn't ask for a moral analysis of the whole enterprise. It's a yes or no question. Do you want to be VP or not?"

"No!" I shouted at him. "No! No!" People turned to stare at us.

"Could you speak up?" he said, grinning. "I didn't quite hear you."

Over dessert two nights later my mother said conversationally, "I finally met the boy who moved in across the street. He seems extremely nice."

"Shane Conner?" I asked, scraping at the bottom of my ice cream dish with a spoon.

"Oh, *he's* Shane Conner?" my mother said. "I didn't know that's who you're always talking about." She looked thoughtful.

"I'm not always talking about him," I protested, blushing.

"Where did you see him?" my father asked.

"I drove by a car wash," my mother said, licking her spoon, "for some club called the Guardians of Democracy."

My father and I groaned in unison.

"What?" My mother looked puzzled. "The sign said it was a fund-raiser, so I stopped and had the car washed."

"Darling, the Guardians of Democracy is a bogus club," my father said. "Besides, I just washed the car on Saturday."

"Hey, how did you find out it was a bogus club?" I said.

My father sighed. "The guidance counselors

are going crazy," he said. "Apparently every kid who joins the club is given the title of 'president' just so it will look good on college applications."

I cleared my throat. "I thought you needed official sponsoring to list something on an application."

"He has it," my father said shortly. "Al Kildaire is the club's benefactor."

I rolled my eyes. Mr. Kildaire is this youngish, leftover-hippie teacher who is just desperate to have kids like him. You know the type: wears a clown costume on Halloween, a kilt on St. Patrick's Day, holds class outside on the lawn when it's over seventy degrees.

"Why are the counselors going nuts?" Pride asked. She's always very interested in anything having to do with high school and the way people behave there. I think she's hoping to have it all figured out before she ever starts.

"Because people who join the club will look just as good as people who have worked really hard," my father explained.

My mother frowned. "I think you're overreacting," she said lightly. "I mean, how many children have actually joined this club?"

My father sighed heavily. "As of this afternoon, five hundred and fifteen."

"Five hundred and fifteen!" I exclaimed. "Two days ago the club didn't even exist!"

"I know, but word is spreading pretty rapidly,"

my father said. "Apparently all you have to do is sign a sheet of paper that Shane has and you're a member of the club."

"Can't you make Mr. Kildaire *un*sponsor the club?" I asked desperately. I thought about poor Katie, who had once spent a semester being abused by the brains in the chess club just so she could improve her college applications. And what about me? What about all the hours I'd spent in marching band, playing flute in the front row with Mr. McDermott screaming and spraying saliva all over the woodwinds? What about my months on the tennis team, freezing in a short skirt? What about all the boring meetings I'd sat through for the National Honor Society while the Latin teacher, Mrs. Ronald, scratched herself with the pointer? Of course, I liked all these activities in a way, but I might not have endured quite so much if it weren't for my applications. And now it seemed I could've led the easy life and still been able to list *Guardians of Democracy, President,* as an activity.

"I'm afraid there's no talking Al Kildaire out of this project," my father said. "He's loving it. He's never been so popular—kids keep thumping him on the back and congratulating him. Plus it seems that Shane convinced him that the club is actually going to accomplish something."

"Well, I'm sure they are," my mother said mildly. "I mean, they were holding a car wash, after all."

"Mom," I said, exasperated, "that car wash is to raise money for them to throw a party."

"Are you sure?" she said, getting up to clear the table. "It seemed quite legitimate to me, and that Shane person talked on and on about good deeds. I gave him an extra five dollars."

I sighed angrily and carried my ice cream dish into the kitchen. I glanced out the kitchen window and saw Shane sitting in his living room, laughing his head off at something on television. Suddenly I remembered that Shane had asked me to be *vice* president of a club where every single other person got to be president!

I stared at his laughing profile, powerless rage heaving inside me. My hands tightened involuntarily, and suddenly I threw my spoon out the open window in his direction. It flew silently, harmlessly, gleaming into the night.

SEVEN

AP ENGLISH WAS mercifully interrupted the next day just as Mrs. McCracken called on me to answer some question about *Beowulf.*

"Knock, knock!" Jubilee Smith called, sticking her perky head in the door. "Carnation Day!"

Carnation Day is this day when you can, anonymously or openly, arrange to have a flower delivered to anyone in school during third hour. The carnations come in three colors: white for friendship, red for love, and pink for secret admirer.

Jubilee wheeled in a cart of flowers. It's one of her many taxing duties as captain of the cheerleading team to deliver the carnations. "Okay, everyone, just hold your horses," she said, checking her list. She made it sound like we were all mobbing around her, clamoring for carnations, when in fact everyone was basically waiting patiently.

You're probably thinking that Jubilee Smith doesn't sound like a real person's name, and you know what? You're right. Her real name is actually Julie Smith, but in the sixth grade she decided that wasn't "festive" enough and changed it to Jubilee. Now ordinarily name changes like that don't catch on very well, but Jubilee went so far as to refuse to speak to anyone who didn't call her by her new name, including her parents.

That's just an example of the kind of person she is. Jubilee's whole life is dedicated to improving her image. Every boy she goes on a date with, she hopes will make her more popular. Every class she takes, she hopes will make her seem more intelligent. Every time she says hello to someone, she hopes it will make her seem more outgoing. Every piece of clothing she buys, she hopes will establish her as a trendsetter.

I know this because I've been in school with Jubilee since kindergarten, and before kindergarten we were in the same preschool, and before *that* we were in the hospital being born together. But despite our shared history Jubilee jettisoned me and all her other friends when it became clear that we weren't going to boost her popularity rating, and now she only speaks to us when we can do her favors.

For example, right now she was reading my

name like she had no idea who I was. "Melanie Merrill? Melanie? Melanie?"

"I'm right here, Jubilee." I raised my hand.

Jubilee trotted down the aisle, her short red cheerleader skirt swishing. "Three red carnations and one white for you, Melanie," she said, depositing them on my desk.

I knew without looking that my carnations were from Katie. Just the same as I knew that Katie was about to get the same from me. It was our long-standing agreement in order to protect each other from the embarrassment of not getting a single carnation. Usually, though, I was the only one who actually needed that protection; Katie always seemed to have a bunch of secret admirers.

"Shane Conner?" Jubilee said. "You have—"

"No, thank you," Shane said lightly from behind me. Brad Hopkins had managed to drop the class after the whole *Odyssey* catastrophe, and Shane now sat in the desk behind me. "I don't care to accept them."

"But you have five red ones," Jubilee protested.

I stared at the flowers Jubilee held out to Shane. He had *five* red carnations? Did he have five admirers or were all five from the same girl? And who?

But Shane didn't seem the least bit curious. "I choose not to accept them," he repeated patiently. "Please give them to someone else."

"But—"

"Please."

Jubilee shrugged. "Okay. Katie Crimson? Katie? Katie?" She headed across the room.

I turned around, genuinely curious. "Why didn't you want your carnations?"

Shane shrugged. "I don't like Carnation Day."

I raised an eyebrow. "What's not to like?"

"I just think it's unfair."

"Unfair?" I said. "To who? Do you mean to poor people? The carnations only cost a dime, and besides, the profits go to the American Cancer Society."

Shane smiled sardonically. "Ah," he said. "So it's all in the name of charity, right?"

I bristled. "It's not just in the *name* of charity—we really do *give* the money to charity."

"Hmmm," he said noncommittally. "Well, tell me something. You're the principal's daughter, so you probably know how much it costs the school to purchase the carnations in the first place. Am I right?"

"Yes, I do know," I said hotly. "We get them from a florist in bulk and the price comes to five cents each."

"Uh-huh." Shane clicked his pen, looking thoughtful. "And how many kids are in the school?"

"Twelve hundred."

"And how many of them actually send these carnations?"

"A lot," I told him impatiently. What was his point? "Maybe—maybe two-thirds."

"Okay," Shane said lightly. "So eight hundred kids each buying a carnation with a whopping five cents going to charity . . . why, that makes—hmm—that makes forty dollars. I bet the American Cancer Society plans its whole budget around that donation," he said mockingly. "Don't you?"

I bit my lip. "Well . . . well, even if it's not a lot of money, it's still better than nothing. It's certainly not *unfair*."

"But if charity's the point of Carnation Day," Shane said reasonably, "why not do something that would make a lot of money?"

"Well, no one said charity was the *whole* point of Carnation Day," I argued.

"Exactly!" Shane smiled triumphantly. "The whole point of Carnation Day is to make popular people feel even more popular and to make unpopular people feel even more miserable."

I narrowed my eyes. "Meaning?"

"Meaning if you have a boyfriend or a girlfriend, you already know about it, right?" Shane said patiently. "You're *already* dating them. So it's not a big revelation to get a red carnation third hour, right?"

"Well, of course not, but—"

"And if you're friends with someone at school, you have lunch with him or her pretty much every single day, right? So that person already knows that they're friends with you before they get the carnation." His bright green eyes were watchful. "And how many times have you actually witnessed anyone receiving a secret admirer carnation?"

"A bunch of times," I said defensively.

"Okay," Shane said. "And who were they received by? The most popular girls in the class, right? Who already knew they were popular and pretty and that lots of poor slobs had crushes on them, right?"

"Will you stop staying *right* at the end of every sentence?" I said irritably as the bell rang.

I gathered up my books and carnations and wandered out in the hall, still thinking about what Shane had said.

In a way he had a point. Carnation Day *could* make some people pretty miserable. Take Pat, for instance. How did he feel on Carnation Day every year, walking around without a single flower, while some kids—the popular kids—lugged around whole bouquets? And what about my deal with Katie? Obviously I was terrified at the prospect of going carnationless and *seeming* unpopular.

Still, it was funny that someone who was well on his way to being the most popular boy in school would think Carnation Day was unfair. In fact, it was hard to imagine that Shane thought of anything as unfair. Was it fair to execute that mass-scale geometry cheat session? Was it fair to deprive Mr. Munger of his cotton candy machine (even if the machine did ultimately make a bunch of kids happy)?

Jubilee passed me in the hall and gave me a big approving nod because I was carrying four carnations. I shuddered. All at once the flowers seemed kind of unappealing. I pictured Shane at his desk saying no to the five red carnations. The image was strong and sweet and strangely moving.

EIGHT

"HI!" SHANE SAID brightly to me the next day when I walked into Mrs. McCracken's class.

"Hi," I said more restrainedly as I sat down. Shane had gotten a haircut and his unruly brown hair stuck up in a couple of places. He looked like he was six years old, tops. I had a strange urge to run my hand through his hair. It looked so soft.

I turned back toward the front of the classroom and tried to brush that thought aside.

Shane leaned forward. "Hey, can I ask you something?"

I sighed. "Can I stop you?"

He smiled. "Who are you going to the Fall Ball with?"

My heart jumped. Was he going to ask me? Then I shivered. *Don't be crazy,* I told myself.

He's probably just gearing up to say something incredibly obnoxious. "I'm not going," I answered quickly. "I never do."

"You never do?" Shane repeated incredulously.

I blushed. What was I thinking to blurt that out? I mean, I never *have* gone, because no one has ever asked me, but I certainly didn't need to advertise that fact to Shane of all people. I cleared my throat. "I don't like—I mean—"

Mercifully the second bell rang, and Mrs. McCracken swept in and began droning on about *The Canterbury Tales,* by Mr. Chaucer.

I slumped in my chair and arranged my face in an expression of careful attentiveness, thankful beyond words that class had started.

But I had to admit, Shane had asked an interesting question: Who was I going to go to the Fall Ball with? Or, since we were in English class: With whom was I going to go?

Of course, it's true that I never do go to the Fall Ball. But it's true just the same that every year, I hope someone will ask me.

Well, not just anyone. The guy I would want to go with, ideally, would be funny and handsome and smart and popular. Of course, we're not talking ideals here, we're only talking about me mustering up some sort of acceptable date. So scratch *smart* off the list because he doesn't have to be a rocket scientist to take me to the Fall Ball.

I guess funny is dispensable too. Okay, that leaves handsome and popular, which is still a tall order for someone who's never even gone to the Fall Ball before.

"What do you mean, you never go?" Shane whispered in my ear. "Does that mean you never go on principle or that no one asks you?"

"None of your business," I muttered, hoping Mrs. McCracken wouldn't catch us talking in class.

"That means no one asked you," Shane said in a low voice.

"People have too asked me!" I whispered furiously.

"Oh, I'm sure they have," Shane said sympathetically.

"Probably lots of friends' older brothers and maybe some of the other teachers' kids and maybe one of your out-of-town cousins who nobody knows—"

"Oh, you don't know anything!" I spat out. "What gives you the right—" I broke off too upset to speak. Is that what I seemed like? Some dreary girl who had to use family connections in order to cough up a date? And how had Shane guessed? It was especially unfair because it wasn't like that—a pity date—with Ben, even though he was my friend's brother.

"Let's not forget the story of the principal's daughter at my old school," Shane whispered, his breath on my neck. "*She* went to the prom with—"

"With her uncle!" I finished, whipping around so I could look him straight in the eye. "I know, I know! But that has nothing to do with me, and if you mention her to me one more time, I'll—"

"Melanie Merrill," Mrs. McCracken said sternly. "Do you have something you'd like to share with the rest of the class?"

I flushed and spun around in my seat.

"Well?" Mrs. McCracken prompted. "We'd all be very interested, I'm sure."

I shook my head. I could hear Shane snicker behind me.

"Very well, then," Mrs. McCracken said. "If we can continue . . ."

I buried my face in Chaucer, determined never to let Shane distract me in class again.

"How do they do it?" Shane asked me after class, falling into step beside me as I walked down the hall.

"How does who do what?" I asked indifferently, struggling with the zipper on my purse. Shane reached over and took my books so I'd have both hands free.

"How do teachers always know when you're talking about something personal and embarrassing?" he said.

I opened my purse, which made a triumphant squeak, and began rooting around for some gum. "What are you talking about?" I snapped. I had decided to pretend that the conversation about my (lack of) Fall Ball date had never occurred.

"Mrs. McCracken," Shane said patiently. "I mean, if we'd been talking about how we hadn't done the homework, she would've said, 'Melanie Merrill, will you please tell us what the Wife of Bath said to the Miller,' or something like that. But since we were talking about your love life, or lack of love life, she did that humiliating do-you-have-something-to-tell-us routine."

I glared at him. I had to admit he had a point, but right or not, he had no business bringing up my love life. Why couldn't he just drop the subject?

"My question," Shane continued, "is how does she know when to say what? And it's not just her. All teachers do it! I have never once in my entire life been talking about something personal in class and had the teacher ask me a question about the reading. And I've never once been whispering about the reading and had the teacher ask me if I wanted to share it with the class."

I looked at Shane. His bright green eyes were practically blazing. I had that strange impulse again to ruffle his hair. I wondered briefly if I was going crazy.

"How do they know?" he said to me. "Do they learn it in college? Do they? Do they?" The bell rang. He leaned closer to me.

"These and other questions," he said mysteriously, and disappeared down the hall, carrying my books, which I didn't get back until fifth hour.

NINE

I PICKED UP the phone that night to call Katie and heard voices on the party line. I heaved a sigh. The Conners were mercifully planning to cancel the party line, but I guess it took a while to hook up their own line.

I almost replaced the receiver, but then I thought, Why not just listen for a minute? I put the phone back against my ear.

"So," Shane said, "are you going to the Fall Ball?"

My heart beat in a jerky rhythm. Was I about to overhear Shane asking some girl out?

"Gross," Marty Richards said so emphatically that I nearly laughed out loud. "I hate dances. Don't tell me you're going?"

"I don't know," Shane said. Then he laughed. "Probably not. The girl I want to ask wouldn't go with me in a million years."

"Well, we'll go bowling or something that night," said Marty, the very essence of comfort.

"Okay," Shane said. "Listen, do you want to come over and watch *Beach Blanket Beauties* on cable?"

"Sure, as soon as I—" Marty said, but I was no longer listening. I replaced the receiver gently.

The girl I want to ask wouldn't go with me in a million years, I repeated to myself as I sat down on the stool at the kitchen counter. I felt my pulse quicken. *Could* he have been talking about me? I pictured him leaning toward me in English class, and I pictured that strange flicker I sometimes saw in his eyes when he spoke to me. Then I remembered his warm hand on my waist at Bobby's party, and I imagined feeling that hand again as we walked out onto the dance floor. . . .

Then I remembered something else: his comparing me to the mousy principal's daughter at his old school.

I hopped off the stool and strode out of the kitchen. I was totally nuts to even think of dancing with Shane Conner.

Despite my resolve, I was still mulling over Shane and Marty's phone conversation when the phone rang after dinner.

"Hello, Melanie? This is Swiss Kriss calling."

I thought it was Katie playing a joke on me, and I can't tell you how close I came to saying something irreparably stupid, like, "Yodelayeehoo!" which would have been the end of my social life (such as it is).

But luckily I hesitated, hoping that it really was Swiss Kriss. I guess that makes me pretty shallow because from what I know about Swiss Kriss, she's not a very nice person. Katie told me that once she was assigned to be Swiss Kriss's partner on some field trip—come to think of it, I believe it was with the German class and they were going to Frankenmuth, which is this really crummy tourist trap of a place in lower Michigan that specializes in Swiss cheese and sauerbraten and Lindt chocolate. Anyway, apparently Katie and Swiss Kriss sat next to each other on the bus for an hour and a half, and Swiss Kriss asked Katie all about herself and Katie was pleased and flattered and sat there thinking, *Why, Swiss Kriss is so charming,* and then when they got back on the bus to go home, Swiss Kriss sat next to Katie and said, "Hello! I'm Swiss Kriss. What's your name?" So much for Swiss Kriss's listening skills and genuine curiosity.

But there's no getting around the fact that Swiss Kriss is extremely beautiful and extremely popular, and if she chose to look up my phone number and dial it, well, hey, I was flattered.

"Hello, Swiss Kriss," I said.

"Hello, Melanie," Swiss Kriss replied. I'll say one thing for her: she's sure to follow the basic rules of conversation, always saying please and thank you and inserting the person's name as often as possible.

"I'm calling," Swiss Kriss continued, "because somebody gave me your name and suggested that you might be interested in working on the Fall Ball committee."

"I'd love to," I said instantly, which was of course a lie. I mean, who in their right mind would *love* to work on the Fall Ball committee? Still, I couldn't help feeling flattered—Swiss Kriss wouldn't call just anyone, after all. Maybe my image *was* improving.

"Great," Swiss Kriss said in her soft voice. "The Fall Ball committee meets every Tuesday and Friday after school. Do you have any questions?"

"Well, just one," I replied. "Who gave you my name?"

"Oh, someone," Swiss Kriss said vaguely.

"Who?"

"Someone," Swiss Kriss repeated, sounding annoyed.

There's no telling how long we might have gone on repeating those two words ("Who?" "Someone"), but I finally realized that Swiss Kriss wasn't protecting anyone's anonymity; she just didn't remember who it was. I'm sure that whatever conversation had taken place about me had blown right out of Swiss Kriss's mind as soon as she'd finished having it. I guess I should feel lucky she remembered to write my name down.

"So, anyway," Swiss Kriss said. "I thought we should have an Alpine theme."

I stifled a giggle. "That sounds good," I said carefully.

"Yeah, well, I thought we could have construction-paper mountains on the walls," Swiss Kriss continued. "And then maybe a giant papier-mâché mountain in the middle of the gym, so that we'd sort of have to *climb* over it to get from one side of the room to the other."

I had a brief vision of some huge class-action suit brought against the school as the result of twenty kids trying to scale a mound of papier-mâché and falling off.

"Maybe we could try to tilt the gym floor," I suggested.

"Hey, that's a good idea!" Swiss Kriss said. "How would we do that?"

I smiled. "Well, actually, I don't think it's even possible, except maybe if there's an earthquake. It was a joke."

"Oh." Swiss Kriss was disappointed. "Still, I'm going to call the custodian and ask him about it. You never know." She sounded a little more upbeat. "Well, thanks, Cynthia."

"Melanie," I corrected her.

"What?"

"My name is Melanie," I said hesitantly. "Remember? You called me?"

"Oh, of course," Swiss Kriss said, unruffled. "Cynthia's just the next person on my list. Sorry. Bye now!"

I hung up the phone and waited for a minute, watching it. I was half convinced that Swiss Kriss would lose her place on the list again and call right back saying, "Hello, this is Swiss Kriss calling. Would you like to work on the Fall Ball committee?"

But the phone didn't ring, so I went upstairs to do my math homework, feeling lighthearted. (And how often does anyone with math homework to do feel lighthearted?)

I, so-called student ambassador, was going to be on the Fall Ball committee. Nobody had ever asked me to do anything like that before. I felt like a starlet being discovered by a Hollywood producer in Schwabb's. Or maybe a lonely alien discovering life forms on another planet—like a whole new world was opening up to me.

TEN

KATIE CALLED ME after school the next day and said, "You won't believe it. The most exciting thing on earth happened!"

I couldn't say anything for a moment, I was so disappointed. It would figure. The most exciting thing in history happens, and I'm at the dentist.

Sometimes I worry that the essence of my whole life can be summed up in that sort of sentence. Like once I read in the newspaper about this girl who missed getting killed in a plane crash because she was home curling her hair! I mean, I'm sure that she and her family were very glad that she did miss the flight, but honestly, don't you just know what kind of person she was?

"Melanie?" Katie said. "Are you there?"

"Yes," I said, still sick with defeat. "What happened?"

"You don't know?" Katie said. "You honestly don't know?"

"If I knew, would I be saying *what happened?*" I said irritably.

"Okay," Katie said happily, warming to her story. "Today we were all in English and you won't believe what Mrs. McCracken was making us do."

"What?" I asked wearily.

"Sing this ridiculous song in Middle English," Katie said with relish. "I mean, you got to follow along with this record of some man singing, but we had to do it *one at a time.*"

"Oh, yuck," I said sympathetically.

"It was *horrible,*" Katie went on. "She called on this one girl, and while she was warbling away, everyone else was looking at each other and basically hoping that the earth would open up and swallow Mrs. McCracken."

"That's awful, Katie," I said, growing a little impatient. "But will you tell me what happened?"

"I'm getting to that," Katie said. "So in the middle of this girl singing, two plainclothes narcotics detectives came storming in and seized Mrs. McCracken's window box."

"What?" I gasped.

"Of course I didn't *know* they were plainclothes detectives at the time," Katie continued breezily. "I thought they were, like, businessmen or something. But then Shane said—"

"Hey," I interrupted. "Please, *please* don't mention his name to me. Do you want me to talk about Highwater—"

"All right," Katie said hastily. "Anyway, you won't believe this, but the detectives confiscated the window box because they said that Mrs. McCracken was growing marijuana in there!"

Wow, I am never scheduling another dentist's appointment during school hours. "Was it true?" I said at last. "Was she really growing pot?" I tried to remember if I'd ever seen Mrs. McCracken water the window box or anything. Maybe I'd be called as a witness.

"Well, I guess it's true because they took off with the window box," Katie said.

"Where's Mrs. McCracken now?" I asked. "Did they arrest her or what?"

"No," Katie said regretfully. "Although everyone thought they were going to. When they led her out of the classroom, she was protesting her innocence."

I heard my mother's voice calling me to dinner. "Look, I have to go. We're about to eat and I want to talk to my dad about this."

"Okay, but call me back and tell me everything your dad says about Mrs. McCracken," Katie said. "And if the phone's busy, it's just my mother talking to my grandmother about absolutely nothing, so call the operator for an emergency interruption."

"Okay," I said, and we hung up.

"Dad!" I shouted.

"What?"

"Where are you?"

"In the living room!"

I went into the living room and stood over him as he lay in his recliner. "Dad, how could you forget to tell me that Mrs. McCracken was arrested for growing marijuana in her window box?"

Before he could answer, the doorbell rang.

"I'll get it," I said, and gave him a significant look. "And then I want you to tell me the whole story."

He sighed.

"Dinner's ready!" my mother called again from the kitchen. I opened the front door. Two men in suits stood on the front porch. It was already dark out, and the wind was beginning to ruffle their short haircuts.

"Hello," I said.

"Hello," said one of them. "We're looking for Martin Merrill."

I crossed my arms. I can recognize a detective when I see one. "Can I see your badge or shield or whatever it's called?" I said.

The man smiled and flashed his badge. I stood aside to let them in.

"Oh, my," my mother said, coming out of the kitchen. She looked prettily flustered. "We were just sitting down to dinner, and I don't like to delay because the baby gets so cranky. . . . Won't you join us?"

She always invites people to dinner, even if she doesn't have the faintest clue who they are. I defy a burglar to break into our house and get out without a dinner invitation from my mother.

The detectives looked at each other. "We really just need to talk to Mr. Merrill for a few minutes and clear something up," one of the men said.

"Well, but aren't you hungry?" my mother argued. "I mean, you must have to eat sometime, right?"

"What are you having?" said Detective Number Two, his hazel eyes flashing. "It smells wonderful."

"Meat loaf," my mother said, smiling encouragement at him. "And baked potatoes and peas."

"And gravy?" he asked.

My mother nodded. "Certainly," she said. "I wouldn't serve meat loaf without gravy."

"That sounds great," the detective said. He told us his name was Detective Marcus and his partner was Detective Kaminsky.

Then he said that he had to wash his hands, and while Joy showed him where the bathroom was, Detective Kaminsky helped Pride set two more places at the table. We sat down to dinner.

"So," I said conversationally, "is Mrs.

McCracken going to be in school tomorrow?"

"Oh, yes," Detective Marcus said. "We never even took her down to the station."

"Really?" my mother asked. "All the mothers at Charity's play group seemed to have heard quite another story. They were saying that she'd been dragged off to jail and so forth."

"Hmmm," Detective Kaminsky said. He was sitting between Pride and Joy. "We just questioned her in the school office and confiscated her window box and took it down to the lab for analysis."

"And what did you find?" my father asked.

Detective Kaminsky looked uncomfortable. "We found enough marijuana seedlings to yield about four ounces of marijuana."

My father rested his head in his hands.

"You don't really think Virginia McCracken was growing pot?" My mother looked amused. She fed Charity a spoonful of mashed sweet potatoes. "We've known Virginia for years, and if there's a more straightlaced—"

"Oh, no, ma'am," Detective Marcus said. "We're pretty sure that Mrs. McCracken didn't knowingly break the law. She thought she was growing geraniums."

"Geraniums!" my mother said. "Where did she get that idea?"

"Someone gave her seeds to plant," Detective Marcus said. "Could I have some more gravy, please?"

Pride passed him the gravy boat. "Can I see your gun after dinner?" she asked him. "Can we go out in the backyard and shoot something? Like a can or a bottle, I mean? How old do you have to be to become a policewoman? Do you want to give me a math problem to solve in my head?"

"Pride, just a moment," my father said. He looked at Detective Kaminsky. "Could I have the bottom line, please?"

Detective Kaminsky sighed. "The bottom line—well, it's complicated. Because regardless of what she *thought* she was growing, Mrs. McCracken was in fact growing marijuana." He paused to take a bite of peas. "On school property, which would make the charge aggravated drug possession."

"I don't suppose," my father said grimly, "that there's a chance you could drop the charges?"

"Well," Detective Marcus said, soaking up gravy with a piece of bread crust, "what we actually came over here for was to see if the school officials would be willing to plead no contest and pay a fine."

"How much of a fine?"

Detective Marcus cleared his throat. "Two hundred dollars."

My father sighed, drumming his fingers on the table.

"Look, I know it doesn't sound great," Detective Kaminsky said hastily. "But we can't just pretend we didn't find marijuana growing on school property."

My father pursed his lips wryly. "I suppose not," he said.

"Can I ask you how you happened to check Mrs. McCracken's window box?"

"We got an anonymous tip," Detective Marcus said around a mouthful of peas. Detective Marcus is the sort of person my mother loves to have over for dinner because he eats third helpings of everything.

My father pushed his plate away, untouched. "I have one last question," he said. "Did Mrs. McCracken remember who gave her the seeds?"

Detective Kaminsky nodded. "Oh, yes, sir." He took a notebook out of his pocket and flipped it open. "A boy named Shane Conner. We're investigating that report."

After the detectives left, my father went into his study for a few minutes. Then he came to the kitchen, where my mother and I were doing the dishes, and said, "Shane Conner and his parents are coming over for coffee and dessert in thirty minutes."

"That's fine," my mother said calmly.

"Fine?" I repeated incredulously.

"What's the problem, Melanie?" my mother said. "We have homemade ice cream and I just picked up some brownies at the bakery today."

"I'm not talking about dessert, Mom," I moaned. "Why do the Conners have to come over here at all? Why don't they schedule a conference like normal people?"

"I suggested that," my father said. "But they're both dermatologists with busy practices and—"

"But coffee and dessert?" I asked. "This isn't exactly a social occasion."

I closed my eyes. I felt like the seer in *Oedipus Rex* (which we read in school last year) who foretells doom while no one listens.

"Hon, will you get the tea service out?" my mother said. She turned to my father. "Martin, why don't you check on the girls and make sure they're doing their homework?"

As I helped my mother arrange coffee cups and ice cream bowls on the counter, I thought that maybe it wasn't so horrible that the Conners were coming over. After all, I reasoned, Shane had seen my family in all its odd glory. I'd had only a few glimpses of his from the window. But now, hopefully, I'd get to see Shane's parents embarrass him to death. Who isn't, after all, secretly ashamed of their parents?

I had just brought down the saucers when the doorbell rang. I set the saucers down and wandered out into the front hall. My father was shaking hands with Shane's parents. "And this is my daughter, Melanie," he said.

I shook hands with Dr. Conner. He was tall, with fluffy silver hair and weathered red skin. Privately I wondered if I'd want someone with skin like that to be my dermatologist.

The mom Dr. Conner (let's call her Dr. Conner Two) looked more like Shane, with the same smooth olive skin and long lashes. She had dark hair, though, where Shane's was light brown.

"Hello, Melanie," she said pleasantly. "We've been waiting to meet all of you."

"It's a pleasure to meet you," Dr. Conner said in a deep voice.

They were disappointingly polite. I wondered how these two normal people had raised Shane.

"Hi, my name is Shane," Shane said, and stuck out his hand.

I rolled my eyes. Thankfully my mother called to me at that moment and I scooted off to the kitchen while my father led everyone into the living room.

"I've dished out the ice cream," my mother said. "I think I'll join our guests in the living room. Could you serve everyone? Oh, and take coffee orders too." She slipped out of the room.

I sighed. Now I had to be family servant. Not to mention Shane Conner's servant. Great.

I set the ice cream dishes and brownies on the tray and tromped into the living room to make the rounds.

"Thank you, Melanie," Dr. Conner Two said.

Dr. Conner took his dish and smiled. I served my parents and then held out the tray to Shane.

He beamed at me. "Hi. Could I have the chicken special?"

For a moment I had a very sharp vision of my cracking my great-grandmother's sterling silver tea tray over his head. Would it damage the tray? Would my great-grandmother's spirit understand?

But instead of sacrificing the tray, I decided to serve Shane his ice cream. I tilted the tray and let the bowl slide onto his lap.

"Oh, hey—yikes," he said, catching it in the nick of time.

"Coffee?" I asked the Drs. Conner brightly.

They both nodded politely, and I went back into the kitchen for the coffee cups. I was trying to decide whether I should bring the whole coffeepot out when Shane appeared in the doorway.

"Excuse me," he said, "but I'd like to speak to the manager, please? Our waitress, a very sullen young woman, hasn't been back to check on our table in quite a while and I'd like some more ice cream."

I gave him a murderous look. "Your waitress is on break," I said curtly. I shoved the coffeepot into his hands. "Carry that."

As usual, he didn't seem to notice my mood. "So what do you think of my parents?" he asked.

"They seem . . . fine," I said, a little annoyed.

Wasn't he at all embarrassed by his parents, like normal people? But he couldn't have been too embarrassed, or else he wouldn't go around actively seeking an opinion of them.

"Most people are really nervous around my parents," Shane remarked casually.

"I can't imagine why," I said loftily, dumping a handful of teaspoons onto the tray.

"Because they're both dermatologists," Shane explained. "My friends always think that my parents are, like, spotting blemishes and stuff."

I studied Shane out of the corner of my eye as I picked up the tray. Did that mean his friends worried *needlessly* that his parents were evaluating their skin? Or did it mean that the Drs. Conner actually *did* critique his friends' complexions?

Shane smiled and leaned closer to me. "Don't worry," he whispered. "I'll tell you tomorrow if they think you need a consultation or whatever."

"Out of my way!" I barked. I brushed past him and into the living room.

"Well," my father was saying. "I asked you to come over because I think we need to discuss Mrs. McCracken."

"This is the dope-dealing English teacher?" Dr. Conner Two asked for clarification as I poured her coffee.

"Well, dope *growing*," my father said. "And interestingly enough, she told the police that Shane was the one who gave her the marijuana seeds."

I took a seat next to my mother and watched the Conners. They looked exceptionally nervous. They'd probably sat through about a million meetings like this one since the day Shane popped into the world. We all looked at Shane.

"Those seeds?" Shane said innocently. "I thought they were geranium seeds."

"I'm sure you did," my father said kindly.

"Mrs. McCracken loves geraniums," Shane added with a proud smile.

"Well, it was very generous of you to give her the seeds." My father paused to stir his coffee. "But then there's the small matter of the anonymous tip that the police received."

I thought Dr. Conner Two's eyes were going to roll out of her head, she looked so exasperated. "Shane, for heaven's sake—"

"Mom, I didn't do anything except give her some seeds," Shane said sincerely. He had opened his eyes very wide. Every kid knows that makes you look more genuine.

"The thing is," my father said smoothly, "that the police tape anonymous phone calls."

"They do?" Shane said nervously. His coffee cup clattered against the saucer.

"Yes, indeed," my father said. "In fact, two detectives were just in this very living room not thirty minutes ago, playing the tape for me, asking me if I knew the person to whom the voice belonged."

My mother and I coughed in unison and then quickly smothered our smiles with napkins. Thirty minutes ago Detectives Kaminsky and Marcus were playing Twister with Pride and Joy. And while that was certainly worth seeing, it hadn't been very dramatic. And certainly no tape had been played, or even mentioned.

"So," my father continued, "while I'm sure that Shane did in fact believe the seeds he gave Mrs. McCracken were geranium seeds"—I had a sudden vision of Mrs. McCracken lovingly, unwittingly watering her window box and almost giggled—"the fact that Shane then called the police and reported marijuana growing on school property—well, therein lies the contradiction."

"What did the detectives say?" Dr. Conner One said. His lips were pressed into a thin white line. "Are they pressing charges?"

"Actually, no," my father said. "Instead we have to pay a fine."

"How much of a fine?" Dr. Conner asked warily.

Even with four other people in the room, I could hear Shane swallow anxiously.

"Would anyone like some more coffee?" my mother said with her typical disregard for climactic moments.

"No, thank you," Dr. Conner said. Dr. Conner Two shook her head.

My father glanced briefly at my mother, then

turned back to the Connors. "Two hundred dollars in fines."

"I see," Dr. Conner said.

There was a long silence. The tension in the room was thick as cotton. Shane just sat there, his face pale, his fingers interlaced on his lap. I was thrilled. Finally someone was going to get the better of Shane Conner! It was too good to be true.

"Well." Dr. Conner turned to his son. "Shane? Do you have any idea how that fine is going to be paid?"

"No," Shane said regretfully.

"Actually, I have an idea," my father said.

I glanced at him, surprised. He was studying his empty ice cream dish.

"I have been having a very busy fall," my father continued. "And consequently I haven't been able to do as much yard work as I'd like. I have trees that need trimming, leaves that need raking, cars that need washing."

I had a horrible feeling in the pit of my stomach.

"If Shane could spend a few Saturdays or Sundays doing that," my father said, "I think that might be worth two hundred dollars."

Shane's eyes widened. "Oh, well, I don't know about—"

"I think that sounds reasonable," Dr. Conner Two said, laying a firm hand on Shane's arm.

"Why don't you plan on seeing Shane here about nine on Saturday morn—" She broke off, looking at me. "My goodness, Melanie. Are you feeling all right? You've turned terribly pale. Do you need some water? Melanie? Melanie?"

ELEVEN

TEACHER QUESTIONED IN DRUG CASE
POLICE BELIEVE RAID TO BE PRACTICAL JOKE

KNOX, MICHIGAN—Yesterday police officers responding to an anonymous tip raided a classroom at Knox High School and discovered marijuana seedlings growing in a window box. More than fifteen plants were recovered.

The teacher, Mrs. Virginia McCracken, claims that she thought the window box contained only geraniums. When told that geraniums bear little if any resemblance to marijuana plants, Mrs. McCracken replied that she would have no way of knowing that since she has never previously succeeded in growing any plants in her window box.

Mrs. McCracken has been cleared of any wrongdoing. Police say that the marijuana seedlings had a street value of less than a hundred dollars.

"It doesn't seem at this point as though we're dealing with a high-school drug ring or anything like it," Detective Arthur Kaminsky told reporters last night. "This is strictly the work of a prankster."

Knox school officials have made no formal statement, except to say that window boxes are now banned in all classrooms.

"DON'T YOU LOVE the way Mrs. McCracken pretended not to know what marijuana looks like?" Shane asked, reading the newspaper over my shoulder. I looked up into his green eyes. "You know she's probably been smoking it for years."

Shane never pretends he's not totally prying or eavesdropping or whatever. Much to my misery, he had wound up being on the Fall Ball committee with me, and we were sitting through one of Swiss Kriss's tedious meetings. I was gaining more respect for popular people every day—the things they put up with were amazing.

I folded the newspaper. "I'm not speaking to you," I whispered back.

"You just did," Shane said, exasperated. "Besides, you have to talk to me. I'm coming over to your house tomorrow."

"Don't remind me."

"Do you want to hear about how Mrs. McCracken called me at home last night?"

"No."

"I'm lying there on the couch, eating a box of raisins, and the phone rings," Shane went on. "I pick it up and this really crabby, sarcastic voice says, 'Is this young Mr. Conner?'"

I sighed. It was hard not to listen to Shane's stories. Nothing ordinary ever happens to him.

"So I said, 'No, this is a drug rehab center; are you ready to admit that you have a problem?' and hung up," Shane said. "But then I was, like, super nervous for the rest of the night that she would call back."

I looked at him. Now that we were on the subject of the seeds, I couldn't help feeling a tiny bit curious about the whole business. "Where did you get those seeds in the first place?"

Shane smiled faintly. "Bobby Weller."

"Bobby Weller!" I exclaimed. I knew Bobby ran with a rough crowd, but still.

Swiss Kriss cleared her throat from the front of the room. "Excuse me?" she said in her soft, pretty voice.

"It was my first day here," Shane whispered, "and I happened to sit next to him at lunch. Bobby said, 'Hey, man, do you like to party?'"

I looked at Shane with reluctant admiration. It's amazing how well he can mimic people. He had Bobby's slow, dopey voice down pat.

"So, anyway," Shane continued. "I thought he was asking if I liked part*ies*, as in, you know, having a bunch of people over or whatever. So I said, sure, I like parties, and Bobby said, 'Well, then you'll like these.' And he handed me this bag of seeds."

"So why did you give them to Mrs. McCracken?"

He grinned. "Well, I certainly didn't want to plant them myself. But I was pretty curious as to what they were."

"Oh, come on," I said bitterly. "As if you didn't know."

"Well, I didn't know for absolute *sure,*" Shane protested. "And I figured, what better way to find out than to give them to Mrs. McCracken? She has that window box full of dead plants. I thought she'd be grateful for a little gardening help."

I looked at him stonily. "And why on earth did you tip off the cops?"

"Oh, just for a little fun," Shane replied easily.

"Fun?" I repeated incredulously. "You could've gotten in real trouble, you know. You're lucky you got off as easily as you did."

Shane patted my shoulder. "I'm glad you're talking to me. What would I do without your words of caution and disapproval?"

I narrowed my eyes. I wasn't about to let him make me feel like some kind of close-minded—well, student ambassador or something. "I mean it, Shane. What you did was totally ridiculous—I'm sure lots of people would agree with me."

"Well, if you'd been around when the cops

came, you wouldn't be saying that." He smiled dreamily. "I'm telling you, it was even better than I'd hoped for. If I'd known about your dentist appointment, I would've waited another day." He edged his chair closer to mine. Our knees brushed, and I felt a rush in my chest. I wished I weren't always so aware of his touching me. I wished I couldn't remember how his hand felt on my waist.

"So, anyway," Shane said. "Why are you on the Fall Ball committee? I thought you never went to the Fall Ball on principle or something."

"Well, maybe I changed my mind."

"Oh, good, someone asked you! Who is it?"

"I said *maybe*," I snapped.

"Hmmm," Shane said. "That means nobody's asked you yet, but you joined the Fall Ball committee hoping to find a lot of other people who are dying to go to the Fall Ball but don't have dates either."

I rolled my eyes. "Have I ever said I was dying to go?" I asked. "Have I? Have those words ever come out of my mouth?"

"No," Shane admitted. "I'm just guessing."

"Well—don't."

"You know what?" Shane whispered. "I can tell you're the oldest child because you're not too good with the snappy comebacks. Saying *well, don't* doesn't really do much of anything other than make me want to tease you more. If you had older brothers and sisters, you'd be better at—"

"Humiliating people?" I raised my eyebrow.

"Exactly," Shane said approvingly. "Now, if you really want to get me back, ask me to tell you the story of my junior prom."

"This may amaze you," I said slowly. "But I don't care what happened at your junior prom."

"That does amaze me," Shane said. "Because I was totally mortified, and I think you would have been pretty pleased."

I glanced toward the front of the classroom.

Swiss Kriss was writing potential names for the dance on the chalkboard in her loopy handwriting. So far she'd written ALPINE NIGHTS, FALL GLORY DANCE, and MOUNTAIN ROMANCE.

"I really think we can do better," she said earnestly. "None of these names are really—well, really *Swiss* enough."

"All right," I said to Shane. "Tell me the story." Hearing his story beat listening to Swiss Kriss, after all.

"Okay," Shane said happily. "I went to the junior prom with this girl I thought was just awesome, and after about the fourth dance she said, 'Hey, you were really with the beat on that one!'"

At that moment my stomach felt hollow. *This girl I thought was just awesome,* I repeated to myself. What kind of girl would Shane think was so awesome?

Shane was watching me. "Isn't that awful?" he

said. "The fact that she said I was with the beat *on that one* is such an insult. What do you think I looked like the rest of the time?"

I straightened my shoulders, collecting myself. "That story isn't as humiliating as I'd hoped it would be. Tell me another one."

Shane shook his head. "First tell me who you're going to the Fall Ball with," he said. "Assuming you do have a date by now, that is. How bad can it be? I mean, we'll all find out eventually, right?"

Swiss Kriss cleared her throat again. "Excuse me?" she said. "I'd appreciate less talking in the back." She smiled gently, looking absolutely beautiful in her pale blue blouse and short skirt. "Now, as I was saying, if your parents have ever been to Switzerland or anyplace close to Switzerland"—Swiss Kriss looked a little nervous here. I wonder if she's ever looked at a globe?—"have them call me to talk about donating their souvenirs."

Shane was still looking at me. "Just tell me who it is, Melanie," he whispered. "I promise not to laugh."

"Why are you so interested?" I asked. "Who are *you* going to the dance with?"

"Me?" Shane asked playfully.

"Yes, *you*," I repeated. I remembered his phone conversation with Marty, and my heart started to pound. "Who are you taking—"

I broke off, suddenly aware that the room had fallen silent and that Shane and I were suddenly the center of everyone's attention.

Shane grinned. "I'm sorry I can't go to the Fall Ball with you, Melanie," he said in a loud clear voice, "but someone else already asked me."

I felt my face turn red. "You—you know I'm not asking—"

"No need to be embarrassed," Shane said mildly. "You should have asked me sooner."

"I didn't ask you at all!"

"Excuse me?" Swiss Kriss said, blinking her large blue eyes. "I think we're losing track of our focus. Please, everyone! Think Swiss!"

I fanned myself with a notebook. At least people were no longer staring at us.

"Why don't you tell me who *you're* going with, Shane?" I said bitterly. "Or is it a secret?"

"Not at all," he replied. "I'm going with Swiss Kriss."

"What's wrong with me?" I asked Katie that afternoon as we strolled toward my house in the bright fall sunshine. Katie was wearing a muted multicolored sweater that her grandmother had knitted for her. She hated the sweater and only wore it for the sake of family harmony. I could never figure out why she hated it, though. To me, it seemed a lot like Katie—beautiful shades of blue and gold and pink.

Katie sighed sympathetically. "Melanie," she said carefully, "I know that you were only trying to put Shane on the spot, but you know what he's like. He never takes anything seriously and he loves to tease you. . . ." She frowned. "Oh, hey, you didn't think he was going to ask you, did you?"

"Of course not!" I said indignantly, blushing furiously. "Why would I think that? Why would I *want* to think that? Have I ever said two positive words about Shane Conner?"

"No," Katie admitted. "I don't think you've ever even said *one* positive word." She gave my hand a squeeze.

"And he's going with Swiss Kriss!" I continued. "How am I ever going to live this down? It would be bad enough if everyone thought I'd asked plain old Shane Conner to the dance, but no, I asked—I mean, they think I asked The Guy Who's Actually Taking the Most Popular Girl in School."

"Well, I wouldn't bet on their actually going together. Swiss Kriss probably won't remember who he is when he comes to pick her up," Katie said, obviously still remembering the Frankenmuth incident.

"Oh, I don't know," I said darkly. "*She* asked *him,* after all—at least that's what he said. I wonder what on earth she sees in him?"

"I know you can't see it, but there is something kind of appealing about Shane," Katie remarked.

"Appealing!" I repeated. "Puppies are appealing, bubble baths are appealing, hot cocoa is—ugh! Now I'm thinking about Swiss Kriss again!—hot *tea* is appealing—"

"I think it's his hair," Katie said musingly, ignoring me. "It's kind of—soft looking."

"Soft looking?" My stomach knotted as I imagined touching his brown, tousled hair. I brushed away the thought. "Why aren't you walking home with Shane if that's the way you feel?" I said with a sniff.

"Look, I said you couldn't see it," Katie added hurriedly. "Anyway, what about *my* Fall Ball problem? What am I going to do?"

I sighed. Frankly, I was glad to change the subject. "Okay, remind me of exactly where we stand. Currently you can't go at all unless you go with Pat, right?"

"Not unless I can think of a really convincing lie about how I have to go to the library in a semi-formal dress," Katie said resentfully.

"Okay . . ." I was silent for a moment.

"Well?" she prompted. "Do you have any good ideas?"

"I have *an* idea," I said cautiously. "I don't think you could really call it a *good* idea, though."

"Oh, tell me," Katie said.

I took a deep breath. "Who's your lab partner in Smiler's class?"

Katie frowned. "Gus Pendleton. Why?"

"How would you like to go to the Fall Ball with Gus Pendleton?" I said, trying to sound enthusiastic.

"What?"

"How would you like to go to the Fall Ball with Gus—"

"I heard you!" Katie interrupted. "But Gus Pendleton? Are you out of your mind?"

"Yes," I replied. "But just for argument's sake, what's so wrong with Gus?"

"Okay," Katie said in a smug tone. "Since I live right behind the Pendletons', I can tell you exactly what's wrong with Gus. He's building a fort in their backyard."

"He is?" I was interested despite myself.

Katie nodded. "Yes, he has all this junk, like lumber and stuff."

"Well, that doesn't mean—"

"*And* he came over and asked my dad if he could have some of our leftover insulation and my dad said 'What for?' and Gus said, *'I'm building a fort.'*" Katie looked at me triumphantly.

I could hardly argue with her that going to the Fall Ball with someone who was building a fort didn't sound all that promising. But it wasn't hopeless either. "Still," I said cheerily, "Gus Pendleton is better than Highwater Pat."

Katie sighed. "Well, I suppose . . . but why Gus?"

I shrugged. "I just thought . . . you know how

Smiler's always hoping that everyone he pairs up will fall in love? And I thought if I talked to him and explained that you and Gus really wanted to go to the Fall Ball together"—Katie groaned and I raised my voice—"then he might, you know, talk some sense into your mother. She'd probably listen to a teacher, after all."

"First of all," Katie said, "and believe me, this is just the first of many, many reasons, Gus Pendleton has never shown the slightest interest in me." Suddenly she began giggling. "Although I guess I could offer to sew pillows for his fort or something."

I laughed. "Maybe you could go there after the dance," I said. "Nice and private and romantic . . ."

Katie moaned. "Listen, Mel, this really isn't funny at all. Can't you come up with something better than that?"

"Well, I'll try," I said tentatively.

"Okay," Katie said. "I'll call you later."

We said good-bye and I went up the walk to my house.

Inside, I could hear Pride chattering away to my mother. "Why can't I talk to him?" Pride was saying.

"Because he's coming to help Daddy in the yard, hon," my mother said. "And I don't want you distracting him."

"Well, can I say hello?"

"Of course."

"Can I ask him, like, five questions?"

"No."

"Why not?"

"Sweetie, I just told you—"

"Well, can Melanie talk to him?"

"Pride, that's different. They know each other from school."

"That's no fair! If *she* can talk to him, so can I!"

I rolled my eyes as I made my way to the kitchen. Imagine someone being jealous of my wonderful privilege of speaking to Shane! I stood in the doorway. "Don't worry, Pride," I told her, "I don't want to speak to Shane ever again."

"Why not?" Pride said. "Because he didn't ask you to the Fall Ball?"

I stared at her. "What are you talking about?"

Pride's cheeks were rosy with pleasure. "Your friend Jubilee called and I took a message and she said, 'Tell Melanie I'm sorry about Shane and the Fall Ball disaster.'"

"You nosy little animal," I snapped at Pride.

"Melanie!" my mother said in a soft, scandalized voice.

"Well, it's true," I exclaimed, suddenly near tears. "And now she won't be able to keep her mouth shut around Shane tomorrow, and—and"—I couldn't think of anything else to accuse my sister of, but I needed to lash out some more—"and she'll probably make an even bigger fool of me!"

TWELVE

ON SATURDAY MORNING a thump against the wall jolted me awake. It sounded as though a baboon on a vine had just flung itself against the side of the house.

I buried my face in the pillow and tried to fall back asleep.

The bump came again. Followed by a muffled slithering sound as though the baboon were working its way along the side of the house. Then there was the unmistakable sound of my window being opened.

I squeezed my eyes shut. *This is not happening,* I told myself.

"Hello, Melanie," said the baboon, who sounded strangely like Shane.

I rolled over. Shane's head was indeed sticking in the window of my second-floor bedroom.

"This has to be a bad dream," I said. I closed my eyes again.

"No, it's real," said Shane.

I peeked. Shane was still there, wearing my father's tree-trimming harness. He had a red bandanna tied around his forehead.

I have to explain that my father has all this professional tree-trimming equipment because Pride and Joy are both afraid of the dark (though they deny it), and if so much as one *leaf* scratches at their windows, they go ballistic and wake my father up in absolute hysterics. So eventually, my father decided it was in the best interest of his eight hours' sleep that he invest in some professional tree-trimming gear and this harness. The idea being that he can climb trees wearing it and if he falls, he'll just kind of hang there until my mother calls the fire department or whomever you call to get grown men out of trees.

But now Shane was using the harness as a freewheeling flying mechanism. He clung to my windowsill like a tree frog.

We regarded each other in silence for a moment—a rarity for him, since he talks so much. What was he hoping I'd do—cry, *Eek, a burglar*?

Finally I said, "You know, breaking and entering is a felony. Try to get into college with *that* on your application."

Shane smiled. "Well, I didn't break anything and I'm not entering." He looked thoughtful.

"But that is a good point." He looked around my room. "Hey, you have a vanity."

"So?"

"My sister has one of those," he said. "I always thought it was a little like having a piece of furniture called *conceit* or—"

"Look," I said. I sat up in bed, keeping the sheet up over my chest. I was wearing another baby-doll nightgown and I didn't want any comments. "Aren't you supposed to be working?"

"I have been working for, like, two whole hours," Shane protested. "And the whole time your little sister stands under the tree and asks me questions and your father hangs out of his bedroom window, saying, 'No, not that branch. Not that twig.'"

"Well, that's what you get for growing pot in class," I said.

The phone rang in the hall outside my room. I glanced in that direction. It rang again.

"Aren't you going to answer it?" Shane asked, grinning.

I hesitated. Why didn't someone else answer it? Why was I wearing this stupid nightgown? Hadn't I learned my lesson that time Shane dropped over for some Drano? I sighed. The phone rang again and I made up my mind. I was not going to let Shane Conner hold me hostage in my own bed.

I threw back the covers and walked over to the window.

Shane widened his eyes and whistled. "Hey, Melanie, that's even better than the other one—"

I slammed the window shut. He barely had time to yank his fingers out of the way. He managed to stay there, clinging to the windowsill.

"Better go answer the phone!" he shouted through the glass. "It might be someone asking you to the Fall Ball!" And then he lost his grip on the sill and skittered off down the wall like a water bug.

Alex Chase was on the line. "Hi, Melanie. Candace Miller dumped me. Do you want to go to the Fall Ball?"

Now this was offensive on several levels.

First of all, just consider the phrasing. I mean, okay, so I'm not Alex's first choice for a date. Does he have to rub it in? Of course, maybe he thought that I had known he was going out with Candace, in which case if he'd said, *Do you want to go to the Fall Ball?* I could have said, *I thought you were going with Candace,* and then he'd have to cough up the embarrassing detail about her dumping him. So maybe he thought he was being really straightforward and aboveboard. Still, don't I deserve a little consideration? A little finesse? Couldn't he have at least put the part about us going to the Fall Ball first?

Second of all, how was Alex so sure I didn't have a date already? I mean, wouldn't it have been just as easy and a whole lot more flattering to call me up and say, *Candace Miller dumped me and if you don't already have a date for the Fall Ball, what do you say?*

And of course there was Alex himself. I remembered his behavior at Bobby Weller's party. I mean, handsome as he was, did I really want to go to the Fall Ball with someone who thinks that *What's green and red and goes around at two hundred revolutions per minute? . . . A frog in a blender!* is a good joke? Still, handsome and popular had been the two qualities I couldn't scratch off my Fall Ball date wish list. I guess I should have been flattered to be his second choice.

But for that matter, how did I know I was even his *second* choice? He could have called half the girls in school before he got to me. In fact, maybe that's why his opening was so hurried. He'd probably spent the entire morning calling girls and saying, *Hello . . . it's me, Alex . . . listen, I was wondering . . . I'm sure you probably already have a date . . . you don't? I find that hard to believe . . . oh, well, Candace and I split up. . . .*

Maybe he was so worn down by rejection that he'd shortened his spiel to *Candace Miller dumped me. Do you want to go to the Fall Ball?* and only then did he decide to call me!

I heard Alex clearing his throat and realized that he was waiting for a reply. What was I supposed to say? I debated between *Listen, pal, an orangutan has more social poise than that* and *I lost all respect for you when you got that lima bean caught in your nostril back in the seventh grade.*

Finally I took a deep breath. "I'd love to," I said.

I ate lunch in my room, since my mother had taken it upon herself to invite Shane to lunch. I tried to tell myself that I was not hiding, I just didn't want to sit through a meal looking at Shane's smiling face. As it turned out, I could have eaten by myself in the dining room since my family and Shane ate outside at the picnic table.

I ate a grilled cheese sandwich and then sat on my bed, trying to lose myself in *David Copperfield* since I had to read it for school anyway.

Voices from the picnic table floated up clearly through my open window.

"I see you're almost finished with the trees on the north side of the house, Shane."

"Daddy, why do you always say north and south instead of left or right or whatever?"

"Because it's more precise."

"Yeah, smart people are precise, Joy!"

I put down *David Copperfield* and drifted toward the window.

"Pride, sweetie, don't *snap* like that," my mother was saying in her gently reproving tone. She stroked Joy's back. "Some people use one and some the other—it has nothing to do with intelligence."

"Thanks a lot," my father said wryly, but he was smiling.

"My father uses north and south, like, exclusively," Shane said. "And frankly, it drives me crazy."

Pride was sitting next to him. "What do you mean?"

"Well, for instance, if you're helping him move something, like this totally heavy chair that my mother keeps making us move from room to room? Just when you're staggering under the full weight of it, he says, 'Careful that the east side doesn't scrape the wall.' And then you have to stop and figure out which way is east while your spine compresses about two inches."

My mother laughed. "I rest my case."

Shut the window and get back to your book, I commanded myself, but somehow I couldn't. I stood at the window, mesmerized, watching everyone eating lunch. It was windy out, and my mother's wavy hair and Joy's soft ringlets were fluttering. Shane was sitting on the end of the bench next to Pride, with Charity in her high chair at the head of the table. He was helping her guide pieces of cheese into her mouth. She's not really a star at depth perception yet.

I couldn't take my eyes off the group at the picnic table. They looked like such a perfect family. They all looked so *right* together—even Shane. All at once he seemed to belong.

* * *

I took a long nap and when I woke up, the house was completely quiet. I looked out the window and saw that the car was gone from the driveway. The whole family was probably off someplace together. Maybe they'd even taken Shane with them. Maybe they were down at the courthouse starting adoption proceedings.

I decided to model my Fall Ball dress in front of my parents' full-length mirror. My mother had helped me pick it out a few days ago—she was in one of her rare extravagant moods, and she wanted to treat me to a dress even though I hadn't been invited to the dance yet.

I got the dress out of my closet. It was a strapless black silk and pretty plain, although it had these slinky sort of detachable things that were not-quite-sleeves and not-quite-gloves, which I pulled over my arms.

I tugged the dress on and nearly gave myself a hernia doing the back zipper. I wiggled my arms into the sleevey things and pattered down the hall to look in my parents' mirror.

I couldn't decide whether the black was a good choice. I had tried on a pale pink dress that was really pretty, and just when I was about to say I wanted it, the saleslady said, "My goodness, you're so pale I can't tell where the dress leaves off and you begin."

Thanks a lot, lady. At any rate, I didn't get the

pink dress. In fact, after that I wouldn't even try on any more pastel dresses, so my choices were red, electric blue, and black. I eliminated red when my mother told me I looked like a valentine. And the blue was so deep that it brought out the blue veins in my pale skin. So I had settled on black, and I liked this dress because I didn't want a lot of frills and lace.

But now as I looked at myself, I thought maybe I looked a little too severe: the black dress, my light brown hair and scared brown eyes, and then all that pallid skin.

But why was I so worried when my date was a boy who'd probably say, *Hey, there's a fungus amongus* and try to pick imaginary cooties out of my hair? If only Alex weren't so hyper. If only his personality matched his looks. Still, no one had to know that I didn't find Alex's hyperactivity completely charming. Maybe everyone would think we were falling in love. Maybe Fall Ball night would actually be magical and Alex actually would fall in love with me and I would have a wonderful calming effect on him.

I sighed. Maybe if I put my hair up, I'd look better.

I piled my hair on top of my head and secured it with a grand total of three bobby pins, which I found on my mother's dresser. A lot of hair spilled out, so I decided to look for more bobby pins in the downstairs bathroom.

I was halfway down the stairs when I heard the unmistakable sound of someone lifting the lid on the cut-glass candy dish in the living room. I froze, clinging to the banister. An intruder? It hardly seemed likely that a madman would pause to eat a peppermint before he slid up the stairs to attack me. A burglar? Stealing the candy dish? Please. I stood up straighter.

"Who is it?" I called.

Silence. The sound of the lid being replaced.

"Who is it?" I called again, my voice a little more tremulous.

Shane walked into view. He was wearing jeans and a T-shirt, with a flannel shirt tied around his waist. His hair had a lot of cowlicks. His narrow face was flushed from the sun and wind.

I sighed with irritation. "Why didn't you answer me?" I snapped.

He swallowed. "I couldn't," he said thickly. "My mouth was glued shut around, like, the world's oldest piece of candy."

"It serves you right for rooting around in that old dish," I said. "I'm amazed you could even get a singular piece out of there; it's all sort of melted together. We only keep it for when my grandfather comes to visit."

Shane was still rolling his tongue around his mouth. "That's why I ate a piece," he said. "Because it reminded me of my grandparents. They have that exact same candy dish, which was this big source of fascination to me when I was growing up."

"Why?" I said absently. My heart was slowing back into its normal rhythm.

Shane brushed some stray locks of hair off his forehead. "Well, first of all, because it's impossible to take that lid off without everyone in the entire house hearing you. It has a sound radius of about half a mile."

"Hey, that's true," I remarked.

"Plus I must've broken my grandparent's candy dish around ten times," Shane said. "It's, like, the opposite of childproof. It's—"

"What are you doing in here, anyway?" I interrupted. "Aren't you supposed to be working in the yard?"

Shane yawned. "I was tired, and your mom said I should just go ahead and take a nap on the couch."

I rolled my eyes. Some punishment this was turning out to be. He was more like the family pet than the gardener or whatever. I guess I'm lucky that my mother told him to nap on the couch and didn't say, *Why don't you go upstairs and stretch out on Melanie's bed? She's taking a nap herself.* What a good thing I didn't come downstairs in a towel or—

"Hey," Shane said suddenly. "Look at you."

I glanced down, conscious for the first time that I was wearing my Fall Ball dress. "Oh, I—I don't just wander around the house this way or anything. I was just—"

"You look great," Shane said. He walked to the bottom of the stairs. "Come here."

"I was just—," I began again, but Shane reached up and took my hand and pulled me the few remaining steps into the front hall.

"No kidding, you look great," he said, tilting his head. "Black suits you."

I looked at him skeptically, waiting for him to begin teasing me. "What—my sunny personality?" I asked sarcastically.

"No," he said slowly. "I guess because your hair is so light . . . you're not going to wear it up, are you?"

I touched the pile of hair on the top of my head self-consciously. "I thought—"

He shook his head. "No, you should definitely wear it down."

"Wait—" I pulled out the three bobby pins. "See? Now it's too much."

"No way," Shane said. "Now it's better." He reached out and fluffed the ends of my hair. His fingers brushed my bare shoulders and lingered almost imperceptibly.

All at once I felt short of breath. I had stood this close to Shane that day in biology lab, but somehow this felt different. The air between us was charged. Somehow it felt wonderful and right to be standing with him, wearing my Fall

Ball dress, feeling his light, warm touch on my shoulders.

"Hey," Shane said softly. "How do you make your hair do those corkscrew things?"

"Hmmm?" I said. "Like that? I just twist it around my finger."

Shane coiled a lock of my hair around his finger and then let it go, watching as it made a loose spiral. "Yeah . . . like that," he said.

I looked up and met his eyes. I could smell the sun and wind on his hair and clothes. It was such a good clean smell. It made me think of fall and leaves and caramel apples and Halloween and bonfires and hayrides and other things I hadn't even thought about in years. For a moment it seemed that my entire childhood was captured in the way Shane Conner smelled as he stood next to me at the bottom of our staircase on that fall afternoon with the bright sunshine streaming through the windows.

Shane was still looking at me, smiling gently, smiling so sweetly that I knew that if I told him what I was thinking, he would say, *I know exactly what you mean.* It was so different from his usual smirking expression that I dropped my eyes in confusion.

Shane's forehead touched mine. Our noses bumped a little awkwardly. I thought, He's going to kiss me, but I didn't do anything to stop it. Shane's lips touched mine very lightly.

He pulled away and looked at me. His green eyes were full of the haunted expression I'd seen only a few times before—only now they were even more piercing, and much more tender. I closed my eyes and Shane kissed me again, more urgently this time. His hands crept under my hair to cup my head.

My mind was swaying. Or no, the world was swaying. Shane was holding me up with the lovely pressure of his hands on the nape of my neck.

I laid my hands flat against his chest and felt a jolt of surprise. He was trembling.

Shane backed me up against the banister. The wooden bars bit into my shoulders, but I didn't care. I put my hand on the back of his head. His hair was as soft as I had thought it would be. If only Shane would never stop kissing me—

The front door blew open and my father came stomping through, followed by my mother with Charity on her hip.

I screamed, probably shattering Shane's eardrum, and we sprang apart.

"For heaven's sake, what's wrong?" my mother said.

"Nothing." I touched my neck nervously. My skin was clammy. "You just scared me, is all."

"Sorry, sweetie," she said. "Did you both have good naps?"

My mother was untying Charity's hood. "Shane? Melanie?"

But we didn't answer. We were too busy staring at each other and smiling the kind of long, slow, secret smiles that are usually associated with couples who have been separated by war or disaster, and then are reunited.

THIRTEEN

"HI THERE," SHANE said softly.

"Hi," I whispered back.

It was Sunday, the day after our kiss, and Shane had come over to wax the car. But instead of getting right to work, he'd surprised me in the kitchen. I had given him half of my grilled cheese sandwich, and now we were sitting at the kitchen table, basically just staring at each other.

I couldn't believe how *right* it felt to sit there with him. Was this really the guy I had spent the whole first month of school hating? Well, okay, maybe what I'd felt wasn't hatred exactly. But he just *got* to me, the way he made me feel so frumpy and fuddy-duddy and principal's daughterish.

Sitting with him in the morning sun, watching him take a long sip of water, watching him watch *me* eat the last of my grilled cheese, I felt anything but frumpy.

Shane reached over and brushed the bangs off my forehead. "Your hair's all shiny in the sun. I didn't think brown hair could get so bright."

I blushed. "Hmmm, bright. That's not a word anyone's used to describe my hair before."

"It's a good thing for hair to be," he said. "Especially if it just gets bright in the sun and if it has those little corkscrew things."

We gazed at each other's hair and eyes and skin a few moments more. Then I became dimly aware of some familiar autumn sounds out in the yard—Pride jumping in a big pile of leaves, my mother telling her to cut it out, those were raked up to be put in bags.

"Maybe you should get to work," I told Shane softly. "My parents might start to wonder."

Shane raised an eyebrow. "Do you really *want* me to get to work?"

I shrugged. "Well, no, it's not that I *want* you to, exactly—"

"You think too much about what people *should* do, Melanie," he said gently.

"That's not true," I said defensively.

He grinned. "Oh, no? Then how come it's so important that I wax the car and bag some leaves? I mean, even your parents seem pretty mellow about it."

"Listen," I said, stiffening, "just because I happen

to think that if you're at someone's house to do yard work as a punishment for planting marijuana seeds in a teacher's window box it might actually be nice if you *did* some yard work doesn't mean that I'm some boring, prissy, policewoman principal's daughter with nothing better to do than—"

"Melanie, Melanie . . ." Shane clutched both my hands. "Who said you were boring or prissy or any of that other stuff?"

You did, I wanted to tell him, remembering all at once everything I'd overheard Shane say to Marty Richards that day in the bathroom. Okay, maybe he didn't exactly say I was boring or prissy, but he might as well have. "Well . . . you . . . a couple of weeks ago . . . I heard . . ."

But I couldn't finish. Shane had cupped my face in his hand. His intense green eyes fixed on mine. "You're not at all boring, Melanie," he whispered hoarsely.

I opened my mouth again, but I couldn't find my voice.

He shook his head and grinned. "You know, I wish I had gone ahead and asked you."

"Asked me what?" I managed to say.

"Asked you to the Fall Ball."

I felt my heart expand in my chest. "You were thinking of asking me to the Fall Ball?"

He nodded. "But I figured there was no way you'd say yes. I mean, you seemed to pretty much hate me."

"Hate you!" I laughed.

He looked at me quizzically. "Hard to believe, huh? I mean, where would I get that idea?"

I blushed. I felt about a million times lighter than I'd been a few moments before. Why had I been so sensitive, anyway? Shane had only been teasing me. And that conversation outside the bathroom—well, I'd probably just misunderstood.

I kicked him playfully beneath the table. "Well, what's Swiss Kriss, then? Your second choice?"

Shane shrugged. "Hey, she asked me. I wasn't about to say no. I mean, what better way to make you jealous?"

"So you're telling me you agreed to take the most beautiful girl in the school to the dance to make *me* jealous?" I asked.

"I agreed to take the girl who some people consider the most beautiful girl to the dance to make you jealous," he replied. "Did it work?"

"Oh, no!" I told him, waving my hand dismissively. "I hardly gave it a single thought till now."

Shane and I were still hanging out at the kitchen table when I heard Pride tramp upstairs about a half an hour later. I had decided not to say anything more about the yard work. Maybe Shane had a point, maybe I did take things a little too seriously sometimes. I mean, what did I care whether the car got waxed? All I really wanted to do was gaze into Shane's eyes.

I was doing just that when Katie stopped by. At the sight of us sitting at the table, she looked a little startled.

"Hi," she said cautiously.

"Hi, Katie," Shane said.

I smiled. By now I was practically bursting to tell Katie what was going on with Shane, but it would have to wait. "Pull up a chair."

Katie sat down. "Listen, the reason I came over is—remember that thing we discussed about Gus Pendleton? Would you still be willing to do it?"

"What thing?" Shane asked. So we had to tell him the whole story of Katie's Fall Ball dilemma and my idea of using Smiler to arrange a date with Gus Pendleton.

"It's not a very good idea," Katie said glumly.

"Hey," I protested, offended.

Shane looked thoughtful. "You don't want to go with Pat?"

She gave him a look. He shrugged. "Okay, Gus it is. I guess I don't really know anything about him."

"He's building a fort in his backyard," Katie said quickly.

"Katie," I said warningly.

"Oh, okay, it's the best idea, at any rate," Katie said. "Will you call Smiler, Melanie? Please?"

How do I get myself into these situations? But I was glad to help solve Katie's Fall Ball dilemma. I dragged the cordless phone and the phone book over to the table.

As I dialed Katie gripped my wrist hard enough to break my hand off. "Be sure you tell him not to mention this in front of the class or anything. Tell him—tell him it would hurt Highwater Pat's feelings."

"Okay, okay," I said impatiently. Smiler's phone was already ringing.

"Hello?"

I cleared my throat. "Could I please speak to Smiler—I mean—Mr. Ramsden?"

I figured I should probably call him by his real name since we were about to ask him a favor, but Smiler said, "This is Smiler."

"Oh, hi," I said. "Well, this is Melanie Merrill."

"Hello, Melanie." He didn't sound at all surprised that I'd called. "Is this about your schoolwork?" Smiler prompted.

"Uh, no," I said. "It's personal."

"Really?" Smiler perked up immediately.

I blushed. Katie and Shane were laughing quietly. "Well, yes, although it's not about me. It's—it's about Katie Crimson and Gus Pendleton?"

"Yes?"

"You know them?" I winced. Of course he knew them.

"Yes," Smiler said again.

"Well, it's just that—that they want to go to the Fall Ball together."

"I'm delighted," Smiler said. "I had hoped they might hit it off."

"Well, the thing is, they can't go because Katie's mom says she has to go with the first guy who asks her, and, you see, someone else already asked her. And we sort of thought . . ."

"Thought what?" Smiler said.

"Thought that you could maybe call Katie's mom and . . ."

"And what?"

I swallowed hard. Smiler was certainly not making this easy for me. "And convince her mom . . . since you sort of set Katie and Gus up . . . we were hoping . . ."

"Oh," Smiler said, getting it at last. "Certainly."

"Oh, thank you!" I said with relief.

"It's no trouble at all, Melanie." He made no move to hang up, and for one horrible moment I was sure that Smiler was going to say, *Listen, I'm a little nervous, do you mind if we do a small role play? You be me and I'll be Katie's mom.* But he just said, "Can you give me Katie's number?"

I gave it to him. "And, uh, could you not mention this in class?" I said. "Because High—I mean, the person who asked Katie first would be really hurt."

"Of course," Smiler said. "I am a master of subtlety."

I debated whether or not to point out to Smiler that anyone who says *I am a master of subtlety* probably isn't.

"Do you want me to call you back and tell you how it goes?" Smiler said.

"No!" I said. "I mean, no, that's okay. I'm sure we'll hear about it from Katie's mom."

"Okay," Smiler said. "Good-bye."

"Bye," I said weakly, and hung up. I dropped out of my chair dramatically and lay on the rug.

"Boy, it's really creepy to think of Smiler having my phone number," Katie said, wrinkling her nose.

I looked at her. "How creepy do you think it is for me to have actually *called* him?" I said. "I'm probably going to have nightmares about it for the rest of my life."

"Well, thanks, Mel," Katie said quickly. "You're the greatest."

"Look, I don't want to rain on anyone's parade," Shane said, "but does Gus Pendleton *know* he's taking Katie to the Fall Ball?"

Katie and I looked at each other, wide-eyed.

So we made Shane call Gus and tell him that he'd heard through the grapevine that Katie would go to the Fall Ball with him if he asked. Of course, he thought that was great. He's probably been in love with Katie for years. Any boy who lived in back of the Crimsons' and saw her all the time would be. I won't bore you with the whole conversation, which was pretty predictable. The only highlight was that when Shane called and asked for Gus, his mother said, "Just a minute, I'll go get him, he's in his fort," which probably gave Katie second thoughts about the whole enterprise, but by then it was too late.

And although for the rest of the afternoon, Shane and I kept saying, "Just a minute, he's in his fort," and laughing, it wasn't very comfortable, because of course we already had Fall Ball dates, and they weren't with each other.

"You seem preoccupied, Melanie," said Mr. Bob, the night manager of Taco Bell.

"I do?" I said absently.

It was Wednesday evening, and I was working the drive-thru window with Mr. Bob because we were shorthanded. I was the only employee Mr. Bob would consent to work with. He thought everyone else was too hyper or irresponsible or not serious enough about their Taco Bell jobs or something. But he liked me just fine. That's what you have to put up with when you have a goody-goody reputation. It's really pretty thankless. I mean, the other people, the ones Mr. Bob thought were such goofs, were in the front, throwing cheese and making fun of customers and having a great time.

"I hope nothing's wrong," Mr. Bob said darkly. His worst fear is that one of his employees will have some personal crisis that will affect their job performance.

I smiled reassuringly at him. "No, I'm fine."

Actually I was thinking about Shane. In the few days since our kiss, I'd been doing that a lot. Right now I was remembering how he'd looked yesterday, when we were studying together in his living room. We were sitting on opposite ends of the couch, our stocking feet touching. Shane's short hair had been rumpled as usual. Even when he was reading, he had the most animated face of anyone I knew. His eyebrows drew together, his eyes scanned the pages quickly, his mouth twisting with private amusement—

"Melanie!" Mr. Bob said reprovingly. A car had just pulled up to the intercom.

"Sorry," I mumbled. I pressed the intercom button. "WelcometoTacoBellcanItakeyourorder?" You would say it like that too if you had to say it as often as I do.

"YesI'dlikeaCokepleaseifit'snottoomuchtrouble," said a voice.

Oh, great, a smart aleck. I rolled my eyes. When are people going to realize that poor slobs like me who have to work at Taco Bell don't have very much of a sense of humor about it?

Mr. Bob popped the cup of Coke and a straw into a bag and handed it to me. I leaned out the window. "That'll be ninety cents, please."

Shane smiled at me from his car.

"Hey," I said without thinking, "I was just thinking about you."

He raised an eyebrow at me. "Oh, really?"

I blushed. Meekly I took his dollar and handed him a dime.

"Thank you, miss," he said in an overly loud voice. "You have an excellent Taco way with Taco customers. I'm sure you have a rewarding Taco career ahead of you. Oh, and you look lovely in that outfit." And he sped away.

I giggled behind my hand. Mr. Bob looked at me darkly, but I avoided his eyes. I wondered where Shane was going. To the library? Somewhere with Marty Richards?

The intercom buzzed again.

"Hello?" I said absently.

"Melanie!" Mr. Bob said in a scandalized voice.

The person in the car began laughing. "Hello!" he called. It was Shane again. "I'm sorry, I thought I was in the Taco Bell drive-thru. I didn't realize that it was a private residence."

I began laughing too, ignoring Mr. Bob's shocked expression. Shane ordered another Coke. I was still smiling after I'd given Shane his second order and watched him drive away.

"Really, Melanie," Mr. Bob clucked. "I thought I could trust you to know better than to have your boyfriend visit you at work."

"Boyfriend!" I exclaimed.

I glanced up at the ceiling and caught sight of my reflection in the huge security mirror Mr. Bob had hung there. Of course I was wearing my army-style Taco Bell uniform and my hair escaped untidily from my stupid Taco Bell cap, but my cheeks were flushed and my eyes sparkled. "Boyfriend?" I repeated softly to myself. Suddenly I felt beautiful.

That night I dreamed that construction men were building an addition onto my bedroom. I could hear the sound of their construction gear and their shouts to one another. One of them sounded like Shane, the other like Marty Richards.

No, over here, the Shane–construction worker said. *I want her to see it as soon as she wakes up.*

That's a real nice romantic gesture, the Marty–construction worker said, *but this thing weighs a ton.*

Okay, that's good, the Shane–construction worker said. *You're still wearing gloves? Good, we don't want fingerprints. . . .*

I rolled over and slid further into sleep.

The next morning I was sitting at the table in my pajamas, shoveling cereal into my mouth in a sort of early morning stupor, when my father said from the living room, "What on *earth* is in our front yard?"

My mother and I exchanged surprised looks. She shoved a piece of bagel into Charity's chubby hands and we rushed into the living room.

"Did you say there was something on the lawn, sweetie?" my mother said. Her face was still prettily puffy from sleep.

"Look!" my father said indignantly. "Look at that monstrosity on our lawn!"

My mother peered out the window. "Where did it come from?"

My father threw up his hands. "I don't even know what it is, let alone where it came from! What are we going to do with it? It's sinking into the grass already. Probably going to tear up the sod—" He glanced at me. "What are you smiling about?"

"Nothing," I said quickly. I drifted closer to the window, rubbing my face gently against the curtains. I smiled into the soft material. The object on our front lawn was the giant bell that had previously sat in the cupola on top of Taco Bell.

FOURTEEN

SHANE DUMPED ANOTHER armful of leaves onto the huge pile we'd been raking all afternoon onto the driveway. "Thanks for helping me rake, by the way."

I threw some leaves on the pile too. "No offense, but I didn't do it to help you out," I said. "This was my Father's Day present to my dad."

"Raking the leaves?"

I nodded. "My dad is one of those people who can never think of anything to ask for so he says he wants homemade presents."

"Oh, jeez, just like my grandfather," Shane said.

"So, anyway, for Father's Day I gave him this ridiculous gift certificate good for one day of raking leaves in the fall, one day of shoveling snow in the winter, that kind of thing."

Shane dropped his rake and stretched. "Doesn't that make you want to take a vow that you will always tell your kids lots of nice, concrete things you want for presents?" he asked. Then he brightened. "Still, it was great of your dad to say that we could have a bonfire with the leaves."

"I know," I said. "That was completely out of character. He's probably inside right now, calling the fire department to put them on call or whatever."

Shane laughed and looked around the empty yard. "Well, I think we're just about through. Should we light it?"

"Sure," I said. I went inside and got the lighter fluid and some matches.

"Melanie," my mother called from the living room. "Be careful."

"Okay . . ."

"I put a thermos of hot cocoa on the counter for you guys," she said.

"Oh, good," I said, grabbing the thermos. "Thanks."

I went back outside, realizing that it was almost dusk. I handed the thermos to Shane and then carefully squirted lighter fluid over our pile of leaves.

I held the matches out to Shane. "Do you want to do the honors?"

He was drinking directly from the thermos. He stopped and wiped his mouth on the back of his sleeve. "Sure."

He lit a match and threw it onto the pile, which flared almost white for a second, then began crackling loudly. The leaves smelled sharp and woodsy.

I sipped directly from the thermos and watched the fire.

Next to me Shane picked up his rake and leaned against it.

He winced. "My back is killing me."

"Mine too." I glanced at him. "Of course, your back might not hurt so much if you hadn't strained it stealing the Taco Bell bell."

He laughed. "Did you see that in the police blotter today? It said that stupid bell is actually worth more than five hundred dollars, which makes stealing it a felony."

"Shane!" I shook my head. "You're lucky they didn't catch you. And that my father didn't ask too many questions. You'd never get into college with that on your application."

"Oh, I don't know." Shane looked thoughtful. "If I were a college administrator, I would want to interview kids who had totally inappropriate things like that on their college applications. I would want to hear the story behind it."

I tried to picture Shane as a college administrator, but my imagination failed me. I studied his profile in the orange light of our bonfire. He looked unfamiliar in the flickering light, and for a moment I felt a little panicky—that strange sensation of being an outsider in your own front yard, when your house is all lit up and you are suddenly sure that if you rang the doorbell, nobody would recognize you.

"Hey," Shane said, "what's the matter?" He smiled at me, and suddenly I felt much better, the way I always felt when he smiled at me.

"Nothing," I said. "I'm fine."

Shane reached for the thermos. "Melanie," he said softly. "I'm really sorry that I told Swiss Kriss that I'd go to the dance with her."

"It's okay," I said quickly. I wasn't quite sure what I was agreeing to—that he was going with Swiss Kriss, that he wasn't going with me, that he was going at all?

"I just don't know how to get out of it," he said. "And besides, you told Alex that you'd go with him."

"I know," I said.

Shane reached for my hand. "But there'll be other dances, right? And we can dance with each other at the Fall Ball, right?"

"Right," I said softly. If Shane had at that moment said he thought we should run away to Mexico together, I would have said "right" in that same breathless way.

"Melanie," Shane said suddenly, "your hands are covered with blisters."

We both looked at my hands. I blinked. "I hadn't even noticed," I said.

Shane smiled. He ran the tips of his fingers very gently over the blisters on my palms. I watched his face in the firelight. How could he have ever seemed like a stranger? I felt as though I'd known Shane all my life.

I leaned closer to him. The fire crackled, his breath was chocolatey and sweet, and I was happy, I was so happy.

On Thursday afternoon I was in the girls' bathroom, putting on lipstick and studying Swiss Kriss out of the corner of my eye. I have to take a moment here and describe what Swiss Miss was wearing: a ruffled white blouse, green leather shorts, green tights, and suspenders. Now if I wore that, I'd look like Robin Hood. Which is not to say that Swiss Miss looked like a normal schoolgirl—in fact, she looked like one of the von Trapp Family Singers—but she looked gorgeous. At that moment my heart sank. I was suddenly sure Swiss Kriss would look so beautiful at the Fall Ball that Shane would forget all about me. I would be stuck with Alex, who would probably (a) talk to Candace Miller the whole time; (b) tell me numerous gross jokes; (c) try to shove a mint up his nose; (d) try to shove a mint up *my* nose—

"Melanie?" Katie said, appearing suddenly at my elbow and breaking into my thoughts. "Melanie?"

"Hmmm?" I tried to calm my racing heart.

Katie was bursting with news. "Did you hear?" she said. "Highwater Pat's having a party after the Fall Ball and inviting the whole entire school."

I blinked. "That's crazy. No one would invite the whole entire school. Not even the *school* invites the whole entire school to anything. You have to have a ticket to graduation, even—"

"I heard it from Bobby Weller," Katie said insistently.

"You did?" You wouldn't think Bobby Weller would be a reliable source for anything, but when it comes to parties, he's usually on top of things. "But the Fall Ball's tomorrow."

"It is true," Swiss Kriss confirmed in her soft, sincere voice. "Apparently his parents just decided to go out of town yesterday."

"Oh, poor Pat," I said. I had never heard of someone as unpopular as Highwater Pat throwing a party. And inviting the whole school! "He must be really afraid that no one will go," I said, thinking out loud.

"Oh, no, *everyone's* going to go," Swiss Kriss said.

"They are?" Katie and I chorused.

Swiss Kriss nodded, frowning slightly at our disbelieving faces. "Yes," she said. "It's going to be totally out of control."

"Out of control?" I repeated.

Swiss Kriss smiled gently. "Yes, because

Highwater Pat isn't, like, anyone's friend. So we don't have to, you know, be careful of his house or whatever. The Highwaters have a wine cellar, you know. We're planning on breaking into it."

I frowned. "Does Shane know about, um, your plans to break into the wine cellar?"

Swiss Kriss looked at me blankly for a moment. "Oh, yes. The whole party was his idea." She turned her attention back to her reflection, applying a thin coat of lipstick to her perfect Cupid's bow mouth. "What do you think of this color?" she asked thoughtfully. "It's called Alpine Red."

"Hello, Melanie," Dr. Conner Two said. She was sitting at the kitchen table, shelling peas.

"Hi, Dr. Conner," I said. "Is Shane home?"

"Yes, he's in his room with Marty Richards," Dr. Conner Two said. "Why don't you go on up?"

"Okay," I said. "Thanks."

I started slowly up the stairs. I wished that Marty weren't here, because I wanted to talk to Shane alone.

My conversation with Swiss Kriss had bothered me all afternoon. I couldn't stop imagining a bunch of popular people deliberately trashing Pat's house—with Shane behind the whole thing. Not that I was stupid enough to give Swiss Kriss the final word on anything. I wanted to give Shane the chance to explain what was really going on.

Now, I didn't *plan* to eavesdrop on Shane and Marty's conversation. But when you hear your own name being spoken through a closed door, it's kind of hard to just knock and ask if you can join in while they talk about you.

"No, Melanie's not the kind of person who would be into that," Shane was saying.

"Yeah, I guess she doesn't exactly go around breaking into wine cellars," Marty remarked.

The two of them laughed.

"Anyway, about this wine cellar business—," Shane began.

"Hey, you know, maybe we won't actually need to break in," Marty said eagerly. "Do you think you could get Highwater Pat to actually let us in?"

Shane yawned. "I think Pat would pretty much do anything I told him to at this point."

Marty snorted. "Yeah, that was pretty awesome the way you just sort of casually suggested we have a party at his place and he went for it. You could be a professional charmer."

I bit my lip. So the party *was* Shane's idea?

"Yeah, that's me." Shane yawned again. "Man, I'm tired."

"Late night with Swiss Kriss?"

Swiss Kriss? I thought, my stomach clenching. Surely Shane wouldn't spend a late night with Swiss Kriss.

"Hmmm . . ."

"I mean, I know it couldn't have been a late night with Melanie," Marty continued. "She's in bed by eight or so, right?"

"Hmmm . . ."

My mind whirled. I waited for a few seconds for Shane to contradict him, but all I could hear was some shuffling around and some soft laughter.

I didn't need to hear any more. I hurried down the hall toward the stairs, my heart thumping. I'd come to confirm that Shane wasn't planning to take advantage of the most unpopular guy at school. What I'd found was far worse than I could've imagined. *She's probably in bed by eight o'clock.* The words pounded in my head. Why hadn't Shane contradicted him? He had told me he didn't think of me as boring or prissy, that he had only been teasing me. But what I heard wasn't teasing—because I wasn't around to tease. What I heard was a calm, rational, mocking discussion about me.

Late night with Swiss Kriss . . .

I should never have trusted him. I should never have dismissed that conversation he and Marty had had outside the bathroom. How could I have let myself like him? How could I have let myself like someone who would take advantage of Pat like this? How could I have liked someone who would take advantage of me?

FIFTEEN

PROMPTLY AT SEVEN o'clock on the night of the Fall Ball, Alex Chase arrived at my house looking extremely handsome in a navy blue suit, and instead of a corsage, gave me a box with a dead mouse in it. Okay, okay, it wasn't really a dead mouse; it was this fake mouse that the Chase family cat plays with. I stared at the mouse while Alex laughed uproariously and then zipped back out to his car and brought in the real flower box. Oh, it was pure class, I tell you.

My mother snapped a photograph of us standing on the front porch. Across the street I could see Shane getting into his car.

"Oh, look, there's Shane," Alex said. "Hey, Shane!"

Shane looked over and waved. Alex waved back. I stared straight ahead.

We got to the dance, and the very first person I saw was Swiss Kriss. She was wearing a short red velvet dress with white fur trim at the neck, hem, and sleeves. Where did she find those clothes, anyway? Did she have some tiny old man laboring away in the Alps for the sake of her wardrobe? Her blond hair was pulled into a graceful twist at the nape of her neck, and no matter what Shane thought of girls who wore their hair up, it looked fantastic. Just the right number of tendrils fell forward to frame her face. Her skin was velvety, her lips as red as the dress . . . I felt like Elvira next to her.

The very first person *Alex* saw was Candace Miller, and he zipped off to get her a glass of punch. I sighed and went to get my own glass of punch.

I stood by the punch bowl forlornly, feeling invisible, like a ghost of past proms. The gym looked beautiful. We'd hung a huge canopy of dark cloth covered with glow-in-the-dark stars from the ceiling, and a mountain-filled horizon wrapped itself around the walls. A couple of corny mountain goats dotted the scene here and there, but even they looked okay in the soft lighting.

I looked around for someone I knew. Jubilee floated by on Brad Hopkins's arm. She gave me a big smile and wave, evidently feeling generous enough to acknowledge me.

After a moment I spotted Katie on the dance floor not far away. She was wearing a short blue dress with some sort of silver sparkles sewn into the material. She had on star-shaped sparkly earrings. Her corn-silk hair looked platinum in this light and the dress was the same blue as her eyes. Gus was looking at her with awe.

She caught me looking and raised her eyebrows very slightly. I knew the look. She was asking me if I needed company. I shook my head.

Pat was here too, wearing a too small suit. He had come stag. I felt a pang of sympathy for him. The Fall Ball was not something you went stag to. Although I supposed I might as well be stag myself, for all the attention Alex was giving me.

Swiss Kriss rustled by in her velvet dress. "Of course Shane and I will be there," she was saying to someone. "Shane planned the whole thing."

I hadn't thought my chest could feel any tighter, but at that moment I felt as though it were filled with knots. *Shane and I.* As though they were an established couple. I remembered the phone conversation I'd eavesdropped on, Shane saying *The girl I want to ask wouldn't go with me in a million years.* Had I actually once thought that he might be talking about me? Of course, he'd been talking about Swiss Kriss. She wouldn't interfere with his plans for a party at Highwater Pat's; with her, he wouldn't have to worry about being *supervised.*

I looked up at the stars on the canopy. I'd spent hours gluing those stupid stars on, stupidly imagining that this evening would be wonderful and romantic.

"Do you have a stiff neck?" Shane's voice said in my ear.

"What?"

He smiled. "You were staring at the ceiling for so long that I was worried maybe your neck was stuck that way."

I turned away and poured myself another glass of punch.

"So where were you yesterday?" Shane said. "I called, but your mom said you weren't home."

"Then I wasn't home," I said shortly.

Shane studied me for a moment. "Want to dance?"

"No, thank you."

He smiled uncertainly. His dark suit and white shirt made his smile seem especially bright.

My hand was shaking. I put down my punch and started walking away.

Shane caught my arm. "What is it, Melanie?" he asked softly. "Are you—are you mad because I'm here with Swiss Kriss? Don't be jealous. You look—"

"It's not that," I whispered quickly.

"Then what?" Shane asked.

I couldn't answer. My vision had suddenly blurred. All the lights in the gym gleamed as my eyes brimmed with tears. *I will not cry,* I told myself firmly. I stared at the floor.

"Melanie?" Shane said. He put his hand under my chin.

Don't touch me, I thought, but I looked up despite myself. I saw him take in my teary eyes and trembling chin and a tiny frown formed between his eyebrows. "Melanie?" he said again.

I leaned toward him. He looked so sincere that suddenly I wanted to tell him everything that was bothering me. "It's about—"

"I really enjoyed our phone conversation, Melanie," Smiler said brightly, appearing out of nowhere with Alex at his side. Smiler was one of the chaperons, which is completely ironic, but never mind. He gave me a big goony smile and walked away.

"Hi, Shane," Alex said easily. "Melanie, you ready to go?"

I looked at him in a daze. My moment of closeness with Shane suddenly seemed very far away and completely unreal. "Oh . . . yes."

"Melanie—," Shane began.

I took Alex's arm, not looking at Shane.

"See you later," Alex said over his shoulder.

I looked at my watch. We'd been at the dance for forty minutes. It seemed like forty hours.

"Do you want to go to Highwater Pat's after we get something to eat?" Alex asked.

I shook my head. "Actually, I'm not feeling very well," I whispered. "Could you take me home?"

* * *

Once I got home, I scrubbed off all my makeup, changed into sweatpants, and joined my family for a late dinner.

I was silent, ignoring the looks my parents were sending me. I kept thinking about the party at Pat's house. A part of me wanted to go over there to run my own damage control operation. But how could I? I might be the principal's daughter, but I didn't have to be a complete Pollyanna.

I sighed. I was reaching for the salad bowl when Charity suddenly banged her tiny fist on her tray. "Go," she said.

I dropped the serving spoon in the salad bowl and exchanged looks with my parents.

"Did she just say something?" my mother said hopefully.

"I don't know," my father said, looking at the baby closely. "Charity? Did you say something, sweetie pie?"

"Go!" Charity said again.

I felt as though a piece of pork chop were stuck in my throat. "Say it again," I said hoarsely.

"Go!" Charity said obediently. Pride patted her back.

My heart started thumping hard. I know an omen when I'm given one.

"I have to go somewhere," I said, standing up.

My father looked surprised. "I thought you didn't feel well."

But my mother only glanced at me and then back at Charity. "I think that'll be okay," she said lightly. "Just don't stay out too late."

"I won't," I said.

I kissed the top of Charity's head, grabbed a windbreaker, and went out the front door. I was running before I'd even reached the street.

Okay, in hindsight it's pretty plain to me that I should've at least slapped on some lipstick before I went over to Pat's. But I felt there were larger issues at stake than mere beauty.

Then again, beauty is one thing and the way I looked is another. My face was pale as milk, without one speck of makeup on it, probably making my eyes look even larger and more frightened than usual. I was wearing gray sweatpants, a ratty sweater that had belonged to my *grandfather,* and a red baseball cap jammed on my hair, which still had a lot of hair spray in it. Okay, are you picturing that? Can you see how gross I looked? Well, then, now imagine who the very first person I saw was when I came chuffing up to the Highwaters' lawn. Swiss Kriss.

She was milling around in the front yard in the midst of a couple hundred other people. I frowned. Why was everyone in the front yard and not in the house? Had the police come already and shooed everyone out? But no, this crowd was too calm.

I elbowed my way through the crowd until I

reached the front porch. Shane was in his shirt-sleeves, ladling out cups of a mysterious punch. Pat stood next to him.

Teddy Inman climbed the porch steps. "Hey, Shane," he said. "Aren't we going to go inside?"

Shane shook his head, handing a paper cup of punch to a girl. He gave her his lightning-quick smile. "Nope," he said. "Pat and I decided to keep things out here."

"But—"

"Hey, anyone need more punch?" Shane called, and was instantly surrounded by people holding out their cups. He tossed Pat a smile over his shoulder.

"Melanie!" I turned around. Katie was standing behind me. Gus was with her. They were holding hands. "I thought you were sick."

"I was," I said simply. I nodded hello to Gus. "What happened?" I said to Katie in a low voice. "I was expecting total chaos."

"I know," Katie replied. She lowered her voice. "When Gus and I got here, there were a few people in the house and a lot of people were out back by the pool. But then Shane came and hustled everyone out and set up those garbage cans on the front porch."

I frowned. Shane set up garbage cans? But I thought he didn't care how trashed the house got—I thought that was why he wanted to have the party here in the first place.

"Melanie? Hello?" Katie said, snapping her fingers in front of my face. "Is everything okay? You look like you're in outer space."

I shook my head to clear it. "I was just thinking . . ."

"So what happened with you and Alex?"

I squeezed her arm. "I'll tell you later," I said. "I have to talk to Shane."

I turned around, but Shane was no longer on the porch. My mind was whirling. I didn't know what to think or what to feel or what I'd say to Shane when I found him. But I made my way through the crowd on the lawn, practically colliding with Swiss Kriss and spilling her punch all over her perfect elfin outfit.

I found him in the backyard, pulling plastic cups and cigarette butts and other scraps of trash out of the Highwaters' pool with a rake. The sight of him stirred up the awful ache I'd felt hearing him talk to Marty. *Don't let him fool you,* I cautioned myself. I'd made a mistake trusting him before—I wasn't about to let my guard down again.

I stood at the edge of the pool. "So," I began, "what's this sudden cleanup act all about?"

He glanced up at me briefly, his green eyes flashing. "What are you talking about? There are a bunch of cups in the pool, and as you can see, I'm picking them up."

"Oh, and I suppose this has something to do with your Mr. Charmer act?" I asked harshly. "You're kissing up to Highwater Pat so that he'll let you raid his wine cellar."

Shane frowned. "You're really losing it, Melanie. I mean, I know I don't meet with your approval, I don't even come close to living up to your standards, but do I have to apologize for cleaning up someone's swimming pool?"

I threw up my hands. "As if this is just about cleaning up! Come off it, Shane—I heard you talking to Marty. I know this party was your idea. I know how you were planning to wreck the place. And I know . . ." The words caught in my throat.

Shane's eyes bore into mine. "You know *what*? What exactly did you hear me saying to Marty?"

My face burned. I tried to control my breathing. "That you were planning on charming Pat into letting you raid the wine cellar. That . . . that . . ."

"That what?" Shane pressed, setting his jaw.

My eyes suddenly filled with tears. "That you'd . . . hung out till late with . . . Swiss Kriss . . ."

Shane's mouth twitched. "That I'd done *what*?"

He stood up and started toward me, but I held out my hand to keep him away.

The tears had begun to roll down my cheeks. A part of me wanted to run home, but I needed to keep talking. "I was crazy to think you actually took me seriously. I mean, all you did was insult me and attack me from the beginning. I'm just one big fat stereotype to you. Just because I'm the principal's daughter, you assume—"

"*I* assume? I assume?" Shane clutched my arm. "As far as I can tell, you're the one who's been making assumptions all over the place."

"What are you talking about?" I asked, pulling my arm away.

"I'm talking about the fact that no matter what I do, you see me as some criminal. You're so worried about people seeing you as some kind of goody-goody because you're the principal's daughter. Well, just because I like to have fun sometimes, you know, pull a few pranks, you have to think the absolute worst of me." Shane's breathing came in short, ragged gasps. His cheeks were flaming. "I mean, you hear a few words out of context and you totally run with them. Did it ever occur to you to ask *me* what the deal was after you heard me talking to Marty?"

I felt a flush of shame. "Well . . . I . . ."

"Marty can be a pretty big idiot sometimes," Shane continued. "*He's* the one who brought up Swiss Kriss, if I remember correctly. I was practically falling asleep. And I'm sorry if I didn't exactly rush to your defense, but frankly, I don't let what people say get to me so much. People can have all the crazy opinions they want as far as I'm concerned."

Shane was standing so close to me now I was sure he could hear my heart beating. Everything he said crashed down on me in dark waves. I thought back to the conversation I'd overheard—what *had* he said exactly? Not much. It *was* Marty who'd done most of the talking. But I'd been quick to blame Shane for everything.

I looked up at him. "Oh, Shane," I said helplessly. "I'm so sorry. I guess . . . I couldn't forget how you teased me about being the principal's daughter. . . ."

"Melanie." Shane stroked my cheek. "You know, it's kind of impossible not to tease you. You're the easiest person in the world to tease—you just get upset so easily." He reached over and tucked a strand of my hair behind my ear. "I never thought of you as just the principal's daughter. When are you going to figure that out?"

I felt my heart swell. "I guess . . . I guess I'm starting to figure it out right this second."

Now, will you explain something I've never understood? Why is it, in romance novels, that the hero and heroine always get together just when the heroine is looking her worst? In *Gone with the Wind,* Rhett declares his love for Scarlett when she's all sweaty and sooty and Atlanta is burning. In *Rebecca,* Max proposes to the narrator just when they've been zipping around in his convertible and her hair is one big tangle. I mean, it's a *book,* right? It's *fiction,* right? The author made it all *up*. So why not have the big moment arrive when the heroine is having a good hair day and wearing some slinky number? For example, it would have been a lot more convenient for Shane to kiss me in the gym, when I had makeup on and was wearing my black dress. But you can't chose where things happen, and if you spend your whole life planning, they might never happen at all.

I looked at Shane for a second, and then I leaned over and kissed him. He seemed surprised, but after a moment he was kissing me back. My arms went around his neck. It was just like I remembered from that day by the staircase. My head swayed giddily, the world turned slowly beneath us. And Shane's arms trembled as though he was very nervous. Or very happy.

I realized then that perhaps this was better than any moment that might have occurred at the Fall Ball. Certainly the stars shining in Pat's backyard were a thousand times brighter, and more beautiful, and real.

Created by Francine Pascal

The *valley* has never been so *sweet*!

Having left Sweet Valley High School behind them, Jessica and Elizabeth Wakefield have begun a new stage in their lives, attending the most popular university around – Sweet Valley University!

Join them and all their friends for fun, frolics and frights on *and* off campus.

Ask your bookseller for any titles you may have missed. The Sweet Valley series is published by Bantam Books.

1. COLLEGE GIRLS
2. LOVE, LIES AND JESSICA WAKEFIELD
3. WHAT YOUR PARENTS DON'T KNOW
4. ANYTHING FOR LOVE
5. A MARRIED WOMAN
6. THE LOVE OF HER LIFE
7. GOOD-BYE TO LOVE
8. HOME FOR CHRISTMAS
9. SORORITY SCANDAL
10. NO MEANS NO
11. TAKE BACK THE NIGHT
12. COLLEGE CRUISE
13. SS HEARTBREAK
14. SHIPBOARD WEDDING
15. BEHIND CLOSED DOORS
16. THE OTHER WOMAN
17. DEADLY ATTRACTION
18. BILLIE'S SECRET
19. BROKEN PROMISES, SHATTERED DREAMS
20. HERE COMES THE BRIDE
21. FOR THE LOVE OF RYAN
22. ELIZABETH'S SUMMER LOVE
23. SWEET KISS OF SUMMER
24. HIS SECRET PAST
25. BUSTED!
26. THE TRIAL OF JESSICA WAKEFIELD
27. ELIZABETH AND TODD FOREVER
28. ONE LAST KISS

THRILLERS

WANTED FOR MURDER
HE'S WATCHING YOU
KISS OF THE VAMPIRE
THE HOUSE OF DEATH
RUNNING FOR HER LIFE
THE ROOMMATE
WHAT WINSTON SAW
DEAD BEFORE DAWN

SWEET VALLEY HIGH™

created by Francine Pascal

Look out for the books now available in the fantastic Sweet Valley High Series

1. DOUBLE LOVE
2. SECRETS
3. PLAYING WITH FIRE
4. POWER PLAY
5. ALL NIGHT LONG
6. DANGEROUS LOVE
7. DEAR SISTER
8. HEARTBREAKER
9. RACING HEARTS
10. WRONG KIND OF GIRL
11. TOO GOOD TO BE TRUE
12. WHEN LOVE DIES
13. KIDNAPPED
14. DECEPTIONS
15. PROMISES
18. HEAD OVER HEELS
23. SAY GOODBYE
24. MEMORIES
30. JEALOUS LIES
32. THE NEW JESSICA
36. LAST CHANCE
44. PRETENCES
54. TWO-BOY WEEKEND
63. THE NEW ELIZABETH
67. THE PARENT PLOT
74. THE PERFECT GIRL
75. AMY'S TRUE LOVE
76. MISS TEEN SWEET VALLEY
77. CHEATING TO WIN
80. THE GIRL THEY BOTH LOVED
82. KIDNAPPED BY THE CULT!
83. STEVEN'S BRIDE
84. THE STOLEN DIARY
86. JESSICA AGAINST BRUCE
87. MY BEST FRIEND'S BOYFRIEND
89. ELIZABETH BETRAYED
90. DON'T GO HOME WITH JOHN
91. IN LOVE WITH A PRINCE
92. SHE'S NOT WHAT SHE SEEMS
93. STEPSISTERS
94. ARE WE IN LOVE?

Prom Thriller mini-series

Thriller: A NIGHT TO REMEMBER

95. THE MORNING AFTER
97. THE VERDICT
98. THE WEDDING
100. THE EVIL TWIN

Romance trilogy

101. THE BOYFRIEND WAR
102. ALMOST MARRIED
103. OPERATION LOVE MATCH

Horror in London mini-series

104. LOVE AND DEATH IN LONDON
105. A DATE WITH A WEREWOLF
106. BEWARE THE WOLFMAN

Love and Lies mini-series

107. JESSICA'S SECRET LOVE
108. LEFT AT THE ALTAR
109. DOUBLECROSSED!
110. DEATH THREAT
111. A DEADLY CHRISTMAS

Winners and Losers mini-series

112. JESSICA QUITS THE SQUAD
113. THE POM-POM WARS
114. 'V' FOR VICTORY

SWEET VALLEY HIGH™

Desert Adventure mini-series
115. THE TREASURE OF DEATH VALLEY
116. NIGHTMARE IN DEATH VALLEY

Loving Ambitions mini-series
117. JESSICA THE GENIUS
118. COLLEGE WEEKEND
119. JESSICA'S OLDER GUY

Rivalries mini-series
120. IN LOVE WITH THE ENEMY
121. THE HIGH-SCHOOL WAR
122. A KISS BEFORE DYING

Camp Echo mini-series
123. ELIZABETH'S RIVAL
124. MEET ME AT MIDNIGHT
125. CAMP KILLER

Dark Shadows mini-series
126. TALL, DARK, AND DEADLY
127. DANCE OF DEATH
128. KISS OF A KILLER
129. COVER GIRLS
130. MODEL FLIRT
131. FASHION VICTIM

Super Thriller Editions
DOUBLE JEOPARDY
ON THE RUN
NO PLACE TO HIDE
DEADLY SUMMER
MURDER ON THE LINE
A STRANGER IN THE HOUSE
A KILLER ON BOARD

Sweet Valley High Super Stars
LILA'S STORY
BRUCE'S STORY
ENID'S STORY
OLIVIA'S STORY
TODD'S STORY

Super Editions
PERFECT SUMMER
SPECIAL CHRISTMAS
SPRING BREAK
MALIBU SUMMER
WINTER CARNIVAL
SPRING FEVER
FALLING FOR LUCAS
JESSICA TAKES MANHATTAN
ELIZABETH'S SECRET DIARY
ELIZABETH'S SECRET DIARY, Volume II
ELIZABETH'S SECRET DIARY, Volume III
JESSICA'S SECRET DIARY
JESSICA'S SECRET DIARY, Volume II
JESSICA'S SECRET DIARY, Volume III
RETURN OF THE EVIL TWIN
THE WAKEFIELD'S OF SWEET VALLEY
THE WAKEFIELD LEGACY: THE UNTOLD STORY

TV Editions
CALIFORNIA LOVE
TWIN HEARTS